Also by *Karla Brandenburg*

The Epitaph Series

Epitaph

The Twins

The Mirror

The Selkie

The Northwest Suburbs Series

Cookie Therapy

Return to Hoffman Grove

Living Canvas

Touched by the Sun

The Mist Trilogy

Mist on the Meadow

Gathering Mist

Rising Mist

Other Novels

Intimate Distance

Heart for Rent, with an Option

Karla Brandenburg

EPITAPH 6: THE SCULPTOR

Epitaph 6: The Sculptor

Karla Brandenburg

Copyright 2018 © Karla Lang

ISBN 978-0-9991213-8-2

This is a work of fiction. Names, characters, places and incidents are the product of the author's imagination or are used fictitiously, and any resemblance to actual persons, living or dead, business establishments, events or locations is entirely coincidental.

This is a work of fiction.

For questions and comments about the quality of this book, please contact Karla@KarlaBrandenburg.com

Cover art by The Killion Group

Acknowledgements

As always, thanks to Terry Odell and Steve Pemberton as my other sets of eyes who help point out what I miss throughout the writing process, and my editor, Kelly Lynne. Special thanks to Dr. Ruth Stoeckel and Dr. Linda O'Connor for speech and medical expertise. Any errors are my fault! And thanks to Bhargav Patel for sharing the walk with me.

Chapter 1

"Hey."

When the man called to her, Maggie Grant dropped her book and jumped to her feet beside the columbarium wall. Built like Paul Bunyan, he was huge—broad and towering. She placed a hand to her chest to still the pounding inside.

On a clear, warm, morning in June, she'd come to the cemetery figuring no one would bother her here. Who was this guy?

"Oh," he said, still several yards away. "I thought you were my sister for a minute. Anything I can help you with?" His voice rumbled deep, like gathering thunder on a humid summer night.

Maggie shook her head and waved him off.

"Genealogy research?"

When she didn't answer him a second time—for fear of sounding like an idiot—his eyebrows knit together. "Guess I'll leave you to it." He raised a hand in the air as he turned away.

He probably thought she was rude, but she wasn't sure how her words would come out, and she wasn't in the mood to either explain or to appear stupid in front of a stranger.

Her last book review for the upcoming edition of the magazine was due tomorrow and she still had a hundred pages to read. And a blog post to write. And social media posts to schedule over the next week.

No one had ever bothered her in a cemetery before.

Her boss thought Maggie's blog was sounding stale, that she needed to find something to wake it up. Maggie had also been told social media directors were easy to replace if relocating to Edgarville meant she'd lose her edge. Maggie had to wonder how many other employees heard the same criticism, a clear indication the boss wasn't happy commuting to a small town.

But Maggie was excited to move to Edgarville, away from Illinois' trendier city of Foxfield where rent was high. In Edgarville, the same amount she paid to her sister as rent could be a mortgage payment for a cottage of her own.

When the man's voice rumbled once more, Maggie raised her head and saw the same giant of a man seated on the ground in front of a headstone. Was he talking to it? Her first instinct was to leave, until she heard one phrase clearly. "I still miss you."

Tears stung her eyes.

Maggie scanned the cemetery and inched toward the man, trying not to be obvious.

She shouldn't be eavesdropping on another person's grief.

The man rose to his feet—he had to be six and a half feet tall, at least. He pressed two fingers to his lips and touched the top of the stone. Maggie swallowed her emotion. His wife?

Without a backward glance, he took long strides down the hill toward the gravel road like Heathcliff crossing the moor.

Heathcliff?

Maggie shoved her laptop into her tote bag, shouldered it, and crept slowly toward the stone to read the inscription. Virginia Carter, beloved daughter. She glanced after the man. No one should lose a child. She looked at the stone again and did the math. Virginia Carter was nineteen when she died—twenty-three years ago. The man didn't look old enough to be the dead woman's father.

Was he her brother? He looked to be around forty. Or had he been the dead girl's boyfriend?

Heathcliff.

Would writing about a man's love for a woman dead that long be an invasion of privacy? She shook her head. He couldn't still be in love with a dead woman, not all these years later, but the idea began to germinate. More thoughts of Heathcliff and Catherine.

She hurried back to the bench and retrieved her laptop, putting her thoughts down before she forgot them. Fifteen minutes later, she packed her things once more. Maggie still had the book to read, but at least now she could knock the blog off her list of to-dos. She crossed to the headstone once more and transcribed the woman's name and the dates in her notebook. With a little research, she might find more to the story, which would give her fodder for more blogs.

Or she'd find out it was the man's sister and there was no romance involved at all.

At least she'd have the one blog post from what she'd witnessed.

She headed to the new Havenswood Publishing building and greeted the receptionist on the first floor. The building still felt empty—other imprints had yet to move in—but *Reading Women* magazine had taken over the third floor. Maggie consulted the desk-sharing kiosk in the reception area for a place to work, and found one—right outside Sloane Booker's office. At times like these, she was glad she did most of her work remotely so she wouldn't have to look at the woman all day.

She rode the elevator up and wrinkled her nose when she got off on the third floor. Fresh paint, new carpet and, underneath it all, freshly brewed coffee. Before she could unpack her tote bag, Sloane called to her.

"Got your draft blog post," Sloane said, waving Maggie into her office. "I think you're onto something. Heartwarming. Really gives the reader 'the feels.' Great story. I think you need to make it a series. Run with it. Can you keep it going all week?"

Maggie gave an internal fist-pump as she hovered in Sloane's doorway. "I think so. I'm planning to do more research on the dead girl today."

Sloane raised her eyebrows. "For real? You didn't make this up?"

"For real," she replied.

"You mean some poor sap is still pining after a woman who's been dead half his life?"

Maggie shrugged. "I don't know the whole story, but I'm looking into it."

"Don't dig too deep. If it turns out to be nothing, you'll lose your readers. You need to schmaltz it up. Make this guy a pitiable character. Play up his emotions."

Sloane's angle hit a dissonant chord. Rather than argue, Maggie nodded and headed for her desk.

"Planning meeting at three," Sloane called after her.

As if she didn't know. Wasn't that why they'd all come into the office today?

Maggie filtered through a box of books to be reviewed on a nearby table. She picked out a couple best-selling authors with new releases and some lesser-known authors whose blurbs showed potential, carried them to her desk, and typed the titles into her online reading tracker. By the time she finished, her computer chimed with the meeting reminder.

Sloane was already waiting at the table while Maggie's coworkers filtered into the conference room.

"Let's get started," Sloane said. "Jean. There's a lot of buzz about the state of the book industry and recent changes. Are you up to speed?"

Jean straightened. "Yes. I've scheduled a meeting with the presidents of two writers' associations for my next article, and I've contacted authors for their perspectives, pro and con."

"Fresh voices? The authors?" Sloane asked.

Jean grimaced. Sloane had needled her in the past about quoting the same stale—she liked the word stale—sources in her articles. "People I haven't spoken with before," Jean replied.

"Preston. What've you got?"

Preston Andrews sat across from Maggie and raised his chin, a show of his typical arrogance. "I'm doing a piece on truth in fiction. Authors who do their research, and authors who fake it and how that affects the reading experience, with a focus on historical."

"Research," Sloane repeated. "Maggie needs to do local research. Maybe you can give her a hand. I see a hopeless romantic angle. A tragic hero who can't get over a dead woman, who goes through every day waiting to rejoin her in the afterlife." She tapped her head. "Maybe he's a bit slow upstairs. Maybe he can't get another woman's attention. Think of the possibilities."

"In which case it might be better suited to Halloween," Preston said.

Maggie tensed. Preston routinely challenged her, which she presumed was to hear her stutter. "It c-c-c-c…" He'd succeeded. She closed her mouth, hit her thigh with a fist. 'Could' refused to form on her tongue. She imagined herself in reporter mode, a technique she'd learned from her speech pathologist. "I want to write while it's fresh in my mind. Besides, he seemed n-n-normal enough. He tried to speak to me."

Preston smirked. He was the type of man who felt his perfect diction made him superior. As a covert stutterer, her speech disorder went unnoticed most of the time, but Preston knew exactly how to bring out the worst in her.

"I don't think people care what time of year it is," Sloane said. "I posted the blog an hour ago and hits are up today. Comments have been pouring in." She turned to Maggie. "I assume you'll respond to them?"

"Of course." She shot an annoyed glance at Preston. "I can manage the research on my own."

Sloane nodded and moved to the next feature writer.

Why would Sloane think she'd need help with the research? Maggie knew her material, knew what she was seeking. The stutter only tended to manifest itself when she was uncomfortable or nervous about something. Maggie *liked* talking to people, and now that she was older, fewer of them noticed—or pointed out—the occasional difficulty. Aside from the passive-aggressive jabs Preston hit her with, she'd overcome all but the occasional hiccups in her speech. She'd learned to become fluent, especially when playing the role of reporter.

There was always a jackhole out there waiting for her to slip up.

Maggie shook herself to pay attention, taking notes of the articles proposed and assigned to prepare social media teasers.

When the meeting drew to a close, Sloane asked Maggie to wait until the room had cleared.

"Just checked hits on the blog again," Sloane said. "People are eating it up. I'm wondering if you should skip the research. Invent a story for this guy and his dead girlfriend to keep it alive. Truth seldom lives up to the fantasy."

"Or, truth is stranger than fiction. I might uncover something more interesting. I want to see what I can find out," Maggie said. "If the truth turns out to be dull and boring, I'll prepare a week's worth of posts ahead of time to keep the momentum going."

Sloane nodded. "Excellent. Nice work."

Maggie returned to her desk and camped in front of her computer. She searched obituaries for Virginia Carter and was rewarded with a local newspaper story on the second page of results. According to the story, on her way home from a party, Virginia drove her car into a house. Maggie blinked several times at the photo that accompanied the article, a sedan parked in someone's living room. How fast would she have to be driving to do that kind of damage? The article went on to say the driver—Virginia—hadn't been wearing a seat belt, went through her windshield and landed at an awkward angle against the living room wall. Her blood alcohol level was well over the legal limit.

Irresponsible. Careless. Or was the accident the result of a one-time mistake? Virginia was young, after all, but was that an excuse?

What about the man Maggie had seen at the cemetery? She didn't know anything about him. Did he have something to do with the accident? The article didn't say anything about passengers in the vehicle.

Virginia had been nineteen. A year out of high school, most likely. Maggie expanded her search to look for a high school yearbook from that time frame. Edgarville was a small town. The class sizes couldn't be big. She might get lucky.

"Nice piece of fiction," Preston said, appearing behind her. "Testing out your novel writing skills on the company blog?"

"Just reporting what I saw," she said without turning around.

"Seems pretty far-fetched to me."

"Does it matter?" She spun her seat to face him.

He sneered. "Not for this rag of a magazine."

"If you d-d-don't like it, why do you work here?"

"D-d-d," he mocked.

"G-g-g." She huffed, unable to get the words out to tell the jackhole to go to hell. "Shut up," she said instead, as she shouldered past him.

"Maggie Grant. Walking thesaurus. You have to think twice as hard as everyone else does, don't you, just to carry on a conversation?"

"Preston?" Sloane called from her office. "Do you mind stopping in when you're done with Maggie?"

"As you wish." He chuckled as he walked away.

Maggie breathed a sigh of relief. She knew better than to engage the enemy.

Chapter 2

As Maggie walked the central business district of Edgarville—two blocks along Main Street—she stopped outside the window of a café. Two women stood near the counter, engaged in conversation. A sign in the window showed public Wi-Fi available.

When she walked inside, the women—one on each side of the counter—stopped talking. Half a dozen tables with faux woods tops dotted the center of the floor and booths lined the windows. The walls were decorated with European travel posters. A bakery case lined the wall behind the counter, beside a swinging door.

On the counter, a display showed a variety of tea bags, including Maggie's favorite blueberry. Maggie took a conscious breath before speaking to avoid the stutter. "A cup of tea, please?"

"You should try one of the apple fritters," the woman on her side of the counter said.

"And an apple fritter," Maggie added. She extended a hand. "Maggie Grant."

"I'm Amy McCormick," the woman said.

"Do you live in town?" Maggie asked. "I just moved here and I'm still finding my way around. I'm looking for a real estate agent."

"Sandra has contacts over at the real estate office." Amy nodded to the woman behind the counter. "Pretty much anything you need is right here on Main Street, but if you want recommendations, feel free to ask."

"Good to know," Maggie said. "But a place to live is my first order of business."

Sandra set the hot water and fritter on a tray and rang up the sale. "The real estate office is across the street," she said. "And I'm here most of the time when you decide what comes next. Feel free to stop in anytime."

"Thanks." Maggie paid for her food, chose a tea bag, and hooked her tote bag on her arm so she could carry the tray. She unloaded her computer onto one of the tables and resumed her yearbook search.

This was a small town. Everyone probably knew everyone else. Chances were one of the women had known Virginia Carter, or the man in the cemetery. Did she dare ask?

Amy waved as she headed for the door. "Nice to meet you, Maggie. Welcome to town."

"Nice to meet you, too, and thanks," Maggie replied.

Sandra came out from around the counter with a washrag to wipe tables. She stopped beside Maggie. "What brings you to town?" she asked.

"Have you heard of *Reading Women* magazine?"

"Yeah. They moved into the Cascade Building, didn't they?"

"That's right. I work for the magazine." This was Maggie's opening. How could she ask without sounding intrusive? "I'm doing market research for the magazine. Can I ask you a few questions?"

"Really?" Sandra glanced around the otherwise empty café. "What do you need?"

"Forgive me, this is an indelicate question, but how old are you? I'm looking for women of a certain age—my age. Right around the forty milepost. You look a little younger?"

Sandra chuckled. "I'm thirty-seven."

"Do you know anyone who might be willing to talk to me? People who might have gone to school here, in Edgarville."

"Amy's close in age," Sandra said. "She's a year older than me. Close enough?"

Maggie's eyebrows rose. "Anyone on the other side of forty?"

"My husband's forty, although he's not likely to read your magazine. And his brother. He's forty-two." She tapped the side of her jaw with one finger. I'm sure there are women, but when you're trying to think of someone, that's exactly when your memory refuses to cooperate. I can let you know next time I see you."

Maggie reached into her bag and pulled out a business card. "That would be great. Or you can give me a call."

A tall, broad hulk of a man walked into the café, a man who looked alarmingly like the man she'd seen in the cemetery. Maggie drew a sharp intake of air.

"Oh, don't worry about him," Sandra said. "That's my husband, Garth. He might look scary, but he's a big teddy bear."

The man swept Sandra into his arms and kissed her. "Who's a teddy bear?" He smiled at Maggie. "How do you do?"

12

Looked like, but not the same man. "Maggie G-g-grant," she said, extending a hand.

"Nice, you scared her," Sandra said, punching his arm. "Maggie just moved here. She works for the magazine that moved into the Cascade Building. Any of the girls you went to school with still in town?" she asked. "She's doing market research about your demographic."

"You make it sound like I'm a hundred years old."

Sandra nudged into him. "I'm a mere babe compared to you old timers."

Garth gave her an appreciative look that indicated he did, indeed, consider her a babe, and not because of her age. "When do we have to pick Zach up from my mother's?" he asked, his voice low.

Sandra tittered and turned to Maggie. "Zach's our son. He's spending time with Grandma today."

Maggie nodded, still struck at Garth's resemblance to the man in the cemetery. Had Sandra said he had an older brother? She held out her business card to Garth. "If you th-think of someone who might be willing to t-talk to me, will you let me know?" And why was she stuttering?

He tapped the card against his hand. "Will do."

They all turned when another customer walked into the café.

"Hey, Pru," Sandra called out.

"Pru graduated between me and Thad," Garth said. "You might ask if she's got a few minutes to chat with you."

The woman had a plump figure. A streak of gray highlighted her sienna-colored hair. "Chat about what?" she asked.

Maggie put on a smile and extended her hand. *Be the reporter.* "I'm Maggie Grant with *Reading Women* magazine, and I'm compiling information on reading habits of different demographics. Do you have a few minutes?"

"I've never been interviewed for a magazine before. Are you going to use my name?"

"Just gathering information at the m-m-m... right now. The article might not run, but if you don't want me to use your name, I won't. I don't expect to ask any questions you might object to. I'm more interested in your reading habits."

Pru shrugged. "Okay."

Maggie invited her to sit and pulled out a notebook. "You've lived in Edgarville all your life?"

"Born and raised," Pru said. "Met my husband in high school, married after graduation. Coming up on twenty-two years together."

"Congratulations." Maggie jotted the information into her notebook. "You keep in touch with your high school friends?" she asked.

"Those that are still around, yes. We don't have any book club meetings or anything, if that's where you're headed."

Sandra brought Pru a cup of coffee and Maggie handed her a five-dollar bill. "On me."

"I'll get your change," Sandra said.

"Keep it for the personal service," Maggie said with a smile. "Much appreciated."

Sandra returned to her place behind the counter and leaned into Garth, huddled in what looked like a more personal conversation.

How to navigate her discussion with Pru to the information she was after? "Are you familiar with the magazine?" Maggie asked.

"Sorry to say, I'm not," Pru said. "But I'll be sure to check out your article."

Maggie poised her pen over the notebook paper. "What kinds of books do you read?"

Pru named off a best seller list, which led Maggie to believe Pru was trying to make her reading choices sound better than they were, but Maggie's quest wasn't to judge the woman based on what she read.

Time to change course. She'd prepared her segue—new girl in town—to see where that would lead. "Is there a theater in town? Where I'm from, we have a place that does movie festivals. They're doing a Stephen King festival now."

"We have to go the next town over for our movies," Pru said.

"Then I guess I'll have to go back to Foxfield. They're running *Christine* this weekend. Did you ever see that one?"

Pru's eyes grew large. "I did. Stephen King scares me." She shivered.

"You don't suppose..." Maggie hesitated, inviting Pru's interest, and then lowered her voice. "I happened on an old newspaper article about an accident here in town. Girl drove into a house. Made me wonder how someone could do that unless the car was possessed." She leaned back and took a sip of coffee. "Although I suppose it happens more often than I'd think."

"You're talking about Ginny Carter."

"You knew her?" Maggie asked.

15

Pru scowled. "Everybody knew her. Footloose and fancy free, that one, with the boys chasing after her all the time. Very full of herself, Ginny was." She pursed her lips. "I shouldn't be talking ill of the dead."

"So that's her buried at Mount Hope? I went there the other day to get some quiet while I was working and I saw a man talking to her headstone. I thought he might be an old beau."

"I can't imagine anyone would care enough to visit her grave, especially all these years later, unless he never had the opportunity to learn the truth about Ginny. She didn't care about anyone but herself," Pru said. "She had a reputation. Took a different guy home every night of the week. She grew up on the wrong side of the tracks, in a manner of speaking."

Maybe Maggie's boss was right and the man she'd seen was mentally challenged. Or a relative to the dead girl.

"But listen to me going on," Pru said, waving a hand in front of her face. "May her soul rest in peace."

Sandra returned with a coffee pot. "Don't listen to her," she told Maggie as she freshened Pru's cup. "She's worried her husband might have been one of those men."

"Don't think we've forgotten about you so easily," Pru shot back at Sandra. "About your mother."

Sandra's eyes hardened. "Rumors are ugly things, Pru. You should make sure you know what you're talking about before you spread distorted stories."

"Just because you finally settled down with Garth Benson doesn't mean people will forget when you lived in the fast lane."

Meow. This interview had taken an ugly turn.

16

"At least I finished school," Sandra said as she headed for the counter.

Pru watched her all the way to the kitchen before she pasted on a self-righteous smile. "Now, where were we?"

"I think we're done," Maggie said. "Thank you, and I'll let you know if they use any information in print."

"Do you want me to spell my last name for you?" She leaned across, reading Maggie's notes. "It's Sawyer."

Maggie wrote it down and Pru nodded. "That's right."

"I appreciate you taking the time to talk to me," Maggie said slowly.

Pru rose from her seat. "I'd better keep moving. Errands to run this morning. If you think of anything else you want to ask, feel free to look me up. Sandra has my phone number."

"Will do."

As Pru walked out of the café, Amy returned. "Where's Sandra?"

"K-k-k." Damn her inability to speak! "In the back," Maggie said.

"Wanted to show her what I found." Amy took a seat at the table and placed a copy of *Reading Women* in front of Maggie. "And I read your blog," she said triumphantly, holding up her cell phone. "That story about the man at the cemetery was heart-breaking. Did you really see him?"

Maggie nodded.

Sandra opened the swinging door from the kitchen tenuously and scanned the dining room.

Amy waved Sandra over. "You have to read Maggie's blog." She turned to Maggie. "No idea who this stranger was? How romantic, or maybe it's just sad. You know, from your description, I'd peg one of my brothers, except none of them has a romantic bone in his body."

"Garth is very romantic," Sandra said.

Garth was Amy's brother?

Small town. What if the man in the cemetery was Amy's brother? His resemblance to Sandra's husband certainly made it a strong possibility. Maggie questioned her decision to write about the man's perceived grief. Her new friends might not be so friendly once they found out.

She could be imagining the resemblance. The man at the cemetery might be a cousin, or not related at all.

"Definitely not Brian," Amy went on. "He's too caught up with Delia these days to be pining around the cemetery." She raised an eyebrow. "Thad isn't the type. I don't even know if he notices women, as a rule. Don't get the wrong idea, I think he just enjoys being a bachelor.

"You know, I spend a lot of time in the cemetery. I sort of work there, so I might be able to help you solve the mystery."

"What sort of work do you do at the cemetery?" Maggie asked Amy, looking for a change of subject.

"My family owns Benson Monuments." She speared Sandra with a look. "And that's all we're going to say about that, right?"

"I've had enough of the past today," Sandra said. "Pru Sawyer was here a minute ago throwing out insults."

18

"I passed her on my way in," Amy said.

"Nothing but love for you, sister," Sandra said.

What was that about?

Chapter 3

Thad Benson carried the engraving orders he'd received to his brother Garth's trophy shop. He needed a break from the cemetery and the nostalgia that seemed to be following him today. As he walked Main Street, the breeze swept over him, like a lover's caress.

He shook off the sensation. He had more important things to occupy his thoughts. After their father's retirement, Garth was discovering how difficult it was to run a monument business in a society where cremation was increasing in popularity. Other monument companies were merging together to share expenses.

When he walked inside Garth's shop, a high school girl looked up from the book she was reading behind the counter.

"He's across the street," she said with a head bob.

Of course he was. Thad thanked her and headed for the café. He looked through the windows and, sure enough, Garth was chatting with his wife, Sandra. Apparently, nostalgia wasn't letting go. Thad was happy for Garth. Truly. But today, the affection between Garth and Sandra jabbed at the empty space inside him.

According to Garth, business at the café had increased thirty percent since Sandra had taken over. She was a savvy businesswoman, and she was part of the family now. Might as well enlist her help with the monument shop since he was here.

Thad pushed inside and cleared his throat. "Got some new engraving orders. Thought I'd bring them over." He met Garth at the counter and handed him the manila envelope before he turned to his sister-in-law. "I know you're pretty busy these days, but I was hoping you could help me with the Benson Monuments website since you're the tech guru in the family. Jazz things up. Improve our web presence to help with marketing."

"Have a seat," Sandra said. "Let me get you a cup of coffee and you can tell me what you're looking for."

Garth pointed Thad to a table, turned a chair around and straddled it. "Rough going with the business?" he asked.

Was Garth bragging that he was a better businessman? Thad forced a smile as he took a seat. "Nothing I can't handle. Still getting used to running the show."

Sandra brought a pot of coffee and sat at the table with them. "I can take a look at the website tonight," she said, "but tombstones and donuts don't exactly reach the same audience. And it is Edgarville. You might consider working with the funeral home and do seminars on pre-arrangements. Take your sister with you. Amy's pretty good at the whole 'final words' piece of the puzzle, and she has loads of empathy and warmth when it comes to talking about that kind of stuff."

She could have said no if she didn't want to help, but she did say she'd take a look. Thad nodded. "Appreciate it."

"Hey, since you're here," she went on, "someone stopped in a few minutes ago. A woman from the magazine that moved into the Cascade Building, She's looking for women of a certain age group—your age group—to talk to. Anybody I can send her way?"

"What magazine?" Thad asked.

"*Reading Women.*"

Garth leaned forward, his chair on two legs, and wagged his eyebrows. "Maybe she's looking for friends."

"I've got more important things to worry about." Thad swatted Garth with the back of his hand and Garth's chair returned to the floor with a thump.

"No one said *you* had to be her friend." The smirk on Garth's face said otherwise.

Thad narrowed his eyes. He wasn't getting drawn into this conversation. The longer he remained a bachelor, the more set in his ways he became. Just because two of his siblings were married and living the dream didn't mean he had to join them, and yet watching the way Garth and Sandra interacted made him think of Ginny once more. It was easy to say his one and only chance had gone to the grave, even when he knew nothing would ever have come from his relationship with Ginny. Still, he missed those long walks to the creek, lying in the tall grass.

"And, since I'm here," he said, switching the subject. "You probably know Old Man Sims passed away last week. His daughter stopped in to pick out a stone. Going to need your help mounting it."

"Just let me know when," Garth said.

"Thad," Sandra said, eyeing him speculatively. "What if you use the website to promote more than the monuments? You sell fountains, too, right?" She paused, as if struck by an uncharacteristic bout of shyness. "And Amy says you carve decorations from the stone scraps at the shop. What about promoting that?"

"It's a hobby," Thad said. "Not sure it's worth mentioning."

Sandra shot a quick glance at Garth before she stared Thad down. "Could be your niche. Just sayin'. You've got Amy and her epitaphs. You could promote the toppers you've added to headstones. What do you call those? Ornaments? Garden statues, too, right? Garth is always worrying that the family business is going to suck you under. Might be your lifeboat. Think about it."

"Garth needs to mind his own business," Thad grumbled, eyeing his brother.

Garth sat back and raised his hands. "Trying to look out for family. You don't need to bite her head off. I happen to think she's on to something."

Thad backed away from the table and grabbed his coffee. "I'll give it some thought. Thanks for your ideas, Sandra."

Ideas he'd forget about as soon as he returned to the monument shop. He wasn't Michelangelo.

Thad shook his head and walked out.

"Wait up," Garth called.

Thad turned in time to see Garth kiss Sandra goodbye—another kick of nostalgia to Thad's gut.

Garth fell in stride as they reached the sidewalk. "Come into the trophy shop with me for a minute."

They shouldered through the door together. The girl behind the counter gave them a cursory glance.

"Take a good look," Garth said.

"At what?"

"Around," Garth said with a sweep of the hand. "Looks different than when Watson was in charge, doesn't it?"

Brighter paint, new display cases, carpeting. He glanced at the ceiling. Fixtures instead of fluorescent panels. "Yeah. So?"

Garth scowled. "The decorating was Sandra's idea. It makes a big difference. She knows what she's talking about, you know."

"I do know. Which is why I asked her to update the website." He gave Garth a shove.

"You willing to give her carte blanche?" Garth rested a hand on one of the display cases. "She can't help you if you aren't willing to make a few changes."

Thad took in the store one more time. Sandra definitely had a flair for decorating. "She wouldn't get too wild, would she? There is a certain decorum that goes with monuments."

Garth raised his eyebrows. "When Dad retired, I don't think he wanted you to let the business die a slow and painful death. This is your time to make it your own. She can do dark and gloomy if that's what your aim is, or she can bring you into the current century and reach a new generation. Your call, but I am kind of hoping there's still a business to pass on to my son when the time comes since you don't seem to be working on an heir apparent. Growing up around the

24

shop with dad and the uncles—those were good times. I'd like to create memories with Zach, hanging out with me and you and Brian."

More nostalgia to pinch his heart. Thad wanted that for his nephews, too, but there might not be a family business to pass on, for the first time in four generations. "She did a nice job for you here."

"And she'll do a nice job for you, if you'll let her. Carte blanche?"

Against his better judgment, Thad nodded. He had to do something to keep the business afloat.

"And you could do a demonstration for the Cemetery Association next quarter. Show off your stonework, the custom stuff, the headstone ornaments."

Thad scoffed. "I don't like show-offs. I'm not going to make a living carving ornaments and garden statues."

"If you want to stand out in this business, you need to show off. You want recommendations? Let the funeral directors know what you can offer. Put together a catalog of the custom work you've done, headstones and otherwise."

"Since you're so smart, seems as if Dad should have left the family business to you," Thad groused.

"You're the oldest," Garth said. "Besides, I didn't want it." He waved around the trophy shop. "I'm happy right here. An extension of the family business, but my own place."

Thad appreciated his brothers—and his sister, Amy—more than they'd ever know, but he wasn't very good at expressing himself. "Let's see what Sandra can do."

Chapter 4

T had sang *Three Little Fishies* along with his niece, Chloe, while he bounced his nephew, Randall, on one knee. He nodded to his mother when she walked into the monument shop showroom. She stopped beside the fountain display, folded her arms, and grinned at him.

"You're a natural," she said as the fishies swam right over the dam for the last time. "Where's Amy?"

"She ran to the store to get some diapers while she had a babysitter." Thad glanced at the clock on the wall.

"Oh, that's right. Kevin's in New York for that Associated Press thing, isn't he?" She held out her arms for the baby as she crossed the showroom. "She could have asked me to watch the kids."

Thad glanced at the clock a second time. "Now's your chance. She should have been back by now. I'm going out to find her, if you'll watch the weebies." He handed Randall to his mother.

"I'm sure she got hung up talking to someone."

"Then I can carry the diapers for her." He tweaked Chloe's nose and she giggled. "Do you mind?"

"Mind?" His mother raised Randall over her head. "Of course I don't mind," she said in a baby voice. "Although I'm sure Mommy's fine, but her big brothers will never stop trying to protect her, will they?"

Randall giggled.

"Protect her from what?" Chloe asked.

"Your mommy knows how to take care of herself," his mother said. "But Uncle Thad and Uncle Garth and Uncle Brian always like to make sure." She winked at Thad. "Go on."

"Thanks, Mom."

In spite of the bullying Amy had endured when she'd been in high school, his mother was right. Amy knew how to take care of herself, and now that she was married, she had a husband to look out for her—except her husband was out of town.

He grinned remembering the way Kevin had faced down Thad and his brothers. Kevin had proven his dedication to Amy, but while he was traveling, someone had to fill in—maybe didn't *have* to, but old habits were hard to break.

Three blocks later, he stopped outside the drug store on Main Street. Amy was talking to one of Kevin's sisters inside the automatic doors. When she noticed him, she walked out, a large package of diapers in her hands.

"Where are the kids?" she asked.

"Mom's with them." He reached for her bundle and she handed him the diapers. "Everything okay?"

"You remember Kathleen?" she said, introducing her sister-in-law.

Thad nodded.

"We got to talking about Kevin's birthday next week. His mother is planning a surprise party. Can you take the diapers with you while I run over to Mrs. McCormick's real quick? Sorry, she's Mrs. Phelps now, isn't she?"

"I could go with you," he said.

Amy put her hands to her hips. "I don't need my big brothers shadowing me everywhere I go, and I happen to know you have work to do. I'll be back in an hour and you can hover over me then. Better still, go hover over my children. They need you more than I do." She took Kathleen's elbow and they walked away.

With Thad holding the package of diapers.

He was proud of the way Amy had blossomed. She'd complained about having one of her brothers lurking around every corner, but Thad knew better. They'd rescued her from more than one awkward situation.

As Thad passed the café, he spared a glance through the window and gave a quick wave to Sandra. He stopped short when he saw the other women seated inside.

Rachel Morrison was huddled over a table with a woman he didn't know. The woman he'd seen in the cemetery yesterday. He was sure she was the same woman. Same big eyes, like saucers. Same wavy flip to her hair, texture against the graceful lines of her face. She had the look of Athena, or Aphrodite, or Hera.

He owed her an apology for startling her, at least that was the excuse he was going with. She was a stranger in town, and like it or not, his curiosity was piqued. Tucking the bundle of diapers under his arm, he walked inside.

"Cup of coffee?" Sandra asked as he approached the counter.

Thad nodded.

The woman from the cemetery had her back to him, her voice clear, a tad on the low side, which gave it a sultry tone that walked up his spine.

"I'm going to guess you like the second-chance tropes when you read, the couples who are parted by distance or circumstance and find their way back to each other," she said.

"I absolutely do," Rachel said. "Don't get me wrong. While it makes for good fiction, there isn't a thing I'd change in my own life. Everything works out the way it was meant to, don't you think?"

More nostalgia. This had been the week for it.

When Sandra handed him his coffee, he cocked his head toward the table.

Sandra leaned over and lowered her voice. "She's the woman I was telling you about. The one from the magazine that took over the Cascade Building. She's doing market research about what people your age like to read."

Thad cocked an eyebrow at her. Was she taking a jab at his age? Not that he was a young man anymore, but he wasn't over the hill quite yet.

Sandra raised her hands. "Her words, not mine. You should talk to her. You fit her demographic."

The woman spoke again, her voice sliding over him like silk.

"What's the name of this magazine again?" he asked Sandra.

"Reading Women."

He took a sip of his coffee. "Doesn't sound like I fit her demographic."

The woman raised her head, half-turned in the chair and looked around the café, but he was far enough behind her that she couldn't see him. Rachel, on the other hand, was facing him. She smiled and gave him a little wave. He returned the gesture.

"Her name's Maggie," Sandra whispered.

Rachel pushed away from the table. "I should probably get going, but feel free to call me if you have more questions."

"Thank you for your time," the woman—Maggie—said as they both stood up. She shook Rachel's hand, watched her leave, then turned around.

He knew the moment she recognized him. Those great big eyes grew larger still. She forced a smile. Was he that scary looking? Sure, Amy called him and his brother troglodytes, but he didn't think that equated to hideous. It was a term of endearment.

Wasn't it?

He took his opening and approached, hand outstretched. "I'm Thad Benson. I saw you at Mount Hope yesterday. Didn't mean to startle you."

"Maggie G-g-grant," she said.

Nerves? Or did she have a stutter? "Sandra says you work for *Reading Women* magazine. Nice to see that office space put to use again. I'd heard the city council had offered perks to get you here. Where did the magazine move from?"

"Foxfield," she said, and then pressed her lips closed, the same way Amy used to when she'd connected someone with a dead relative, a sure sign she was uncomfortable.

Unbidden, a protective reflex kicked in, which he tried to tamp down. "Foxfield," he repeated. "Pretty big city, isn't it? Must be somewhat of a culture shock to move to Edgarville."

She nodded and his protective reflex fought to be acknowledged once more.

Was he that intimidating?

He circled back to why she was at the cemetery. "You have family here?" he asked.

She shook her head, rapped a fist against her thigh, cast a 'help me' glance at Sandra.

He got the hint. She'd been chatting away with Rachel like old friends. Now she couldn't speak? Clearly, there was something about him that made her uncomfortable. No surprise there. Wouldn't be the first time his face frightened someone.

He raised his coffee cup. "Guess I should be going. Nice to meet you, Maggie."

Her eyes darted to the diapers under his arm. "You, t-t-t..." Fist to the thigh again. "Same," she said.

Thad shot a parting glance at Sandra and walked out of the café, nearly running into Rachel.

"Almost got a shirt full of coffee," he joked. "How you doing, Rachel?"

"Good to see you, Thad. Been a long time. How are things at the monument shop? I hear you took over from your dad."

"Still getting comfortable at the helm," he said. "I see you met Maggie."

"She's sweet, isn't she? She says she does book reviews for the magazine, mostly, and she apparently writes a blog. She said she's the social media director there."

He glanced through the window. "Sandra says she's doing market research."

"I'm sure she'd love to talk to you about it. Did you introduce yourself?"

Maggie walked out of the café and headed the opposite direction.

"Between you and me, I think I make her nervous."

"You?" Rachel asked. She leaned in to whisper. "I get the idea she's unattached. Those nerves might mean she thinks you're cute."

Cute? Thad laughed out loud. "You do mean ruggedly handsome, don't you? Emphasis on the rugged. Very rugged."

"Don't go looking for compliments from me," Rachel teased. "I'm a happily married woman these days which, of course, does not preclude me from playing matchmaker."

"Don't try too hard. Even if I wasn't a confirmed bachelor—which I am—the lady looked more frightened of me than attracted." He winked.

"Modesty doesn't become you, Thad Benson," Rachel said with a gentle squeeze to his arm. "And you never know when Ms. Right might walk into your life and change your mind."

Thad laughed again. "Pretty sure my shelf life has expired, but thanks for your confidence." He tipped two fingers to his brow and set his course for the monument shop.

Chapter 5

With a cup of tea and a turkey wrap in hand, Maggie chose the farthest table from the counter to wait for Jean to join her for lunch.

Tuesday. Book club night. Maggie dialed her sister to check in.

"I have to say, it's awful quiet around the house without you there," Torie said when she answered.

"No one wants to listen to you and the current boyfriend having sex," Maggie teased.

"As if," Torie laughed. "You've totally ruined my excuse for not inviting him to our place. It's so much easier if I can go to his place and make up a reason why I have to leave. If he comes to our house, he'd never go home."

"Thou dost protest too much." Maggie laughed. "But I do miss you."

"Then don't move so far away."

"You need your space as much as I do," Maggie said. "I sort of got the idea you might like to invite the current boyfriend home sometimes. Not that I don't mind watching television with the two of you, like a flat third wheel…"

"Never flat," Torie joked. "You are coming to book club tonight, aren't you?"

Jean walked into the café and Maggie waved to her. Jean returned the wave and continued to the counter.

"Of course I'm coming to book club," she replied. "What would you think if I invite a couple of new people? Friends I've met here in Edgarville?"

"The more the merrier. Make sure they know to bring a bottle of wine." She paused. "New friends, huh. Please don't tell me they're luring you to stay there."

"You know I want a place of my own, and at my age, I should have had one long ago." She took a sip of tea, closed her eyes and sighed. "You'll never guess what I'm having with my lunch, in the downtown café."

"I can't imagine."

"Blueberry tea! The grocery store doesn't carry it, but the café manager has a delightful assortment of tea bags in the café. She might win me over." She nodded as Jean approached the table with her lunch. "Listen, Jean just got here. I'm going to let you go and I'll see you tonight."

"At which time I'm going to remind you of all the reasons you should stay in Foxfield."

"It's only a forty-five-minute drive," Maggie said.

"Say hi to Jean. I'll see you tonight."

"Girl, I read today's blog," Jean gushed when Maggie set her phone down. "Sloane is through the roof excited about the number of hits you're getting!"

"I promised her a week's worth of Haunted Heathcliff," Maggie replied.

Jean put a hand to her heart and raised her eyes heavenward. "Perfect. That so describes him. The poor man's Catherine is dead and he doesn't know how to carry on without her."

Maggie shot a nervous look toward Sandra and lowered her voice. "Small town, so we should probably keep our voices down."

"Oh, right. Gotcha." Jean took a bite of her sandwich. "So what have you found out?" she asked between bites.

Maggie glanced at Sandra again and scooted her chair closer to Jean's. "A lot. Small town."

"Tell me everything."

"I'd better not. Everyone seems to be related to everyone else, and I'm starting to feel guilty that I eavesdropped on such a private conversation, if you know what I mean."

"You made new friends, already? Leave it to you. And now you're worried you're going to offend them."

"Which reminds me. I was thinking of inviting a couple of them to book club tonight. Sandra," she said nodding to where the woman in question stood behind the counter, "and Amy. Her sister-in-law. But then we can't talk about Haunted Heathcliff, okay?"

Jean gasped. "Wait a minute. You met this guy? Is that what you're telling me?"

Maggie put a finger to her lips to encourage Jean to speak more softly.

Jean hunched over the table. "So is he a few brain cells short? Or is he a dreamy, romantic hero?"

"He seems smart enough," Maggie replied.

Jean rounded her shoulders and rubbed her hands together. "Which leaves..."

"Intruding on someone else's privacy."

"At least tell me what he looks like."

Maggie sat back, picturing her close encounter with Thad Benson. "He's a big guy. Tall. Broad. His hair is sort of medium brown and he has amber-colored eyes that remind me of marbles. Amiable sort, as far as I can tell."

"Married?" Jean asked.

Maggie shot another nervous glance at Sandra, who was engrossed in conversation with another customer at the counter.

"Might be. He was carrying diapers when I met him. Although, if you were married, would you be telling a dead girl you missed her?"

Jean pointed a finger at Maggie and winked. "Good point."

"How's your article coming along?"

"To quote our favorite editor, it feels very stale. I *am* talking to fresh voices, but I feel like the topic has been covered to death." Jean shrugged. "It's what Sloane wanted." She took a bite of her wrap, and washed it down with a sip of her soft drink.

"Yeah, Sloane doesn't seem too happy with the move. She's making everyone's lives miserable." Maggie nursed her tea, staring into the cup. "You think the blog readers will be content with a fictionalized version of the man in the cemetery rather than the facts? I'm wondering how that will float with Preston's Truth in Fiction piece."

"Preston's an asshole. The audience we reach will eat it up." She took another bite. "Why? Is the truth inconvenient?"

"To say the least. I've talked to a couple of the locals, and the dead girl was popular with the wrong crowd, and not very popular among her female peers."

Jean took another sip of her drink. "Jealousy."

"Partly, but from the sounds of it, they had reason to be jealous."

Jean glanced around the café, lowering her voice again. "Maneater?"

Maggie nodded. "Twenty-three years ago, which would provide her with a different sort of label."

"And the guy?"

"Maybe he's a do-gooder. Or maybe she had special talents he hasn't found somewhere else, if you know what I mean." Maggie wagged her eyebrows.

"Twenty-three years is a long time to fantasize about the perfect blow job." Jean's straw slurped at the bottom of her cup. "I have to get back to the office. I have a phone interview with one of those writer groups in half an hour." She glanced around the café once more. "This is a great spot, though. Beats the deli at work, hands-down. I predict these folks are going to do a booming business once word gets out in the office."

"I think she's already doing a pretty good business," Maggie said, watching the beginnings of a lunch rush at the counter. "So new book club members, yay or nay?"

"Yay." Jean leaned over and gave Maggie a hug before she dashed out. "See you tonight."

Maggie pulled out her laptop to write tomorrow's blog post. She'd promised Sloane seven posts, two of which had already run, but the more she found out about Virginia Carter, the more she sympathized with Thad Benson. Had Virginia been so beautiful that she could blind an otherwise reasonable man?

How reasonable could he be? Maggie had been so moved by his affection for this clearly unworthy dead girl that she didn't know what to think of him.

Devoted? Or desperately misguided? Were the women she'd spoken to jealous?

What if Virginia did love Thad? Maybe he knew something those women didn't.

She typed her thoughts, leaving out the names as she speculated, choosing her words carefully.

And then she heard his voice again, a rumble that crept across the floor and resonated inside her. Maggie looked up.

Jean had asked what he looked like. Maggie had given her the basics, but she'd left out the crease in his cheek when he smiled, the laugh lines around his eyes, the square cut of his jaw, the dent in the tip of his nose and, of course, there was his voice.

What would it be like to have someone still be in love with you, twenty-three years later? He had to be romanticizing his relationship with Virginia Carter, forgetting the bad things in favor of the good. People did that all the time when they lost someone they cared about, and even when they lost someone they didn't care so much about. Did he really love Virginia? Or was it a convenient memory?

"Nice to see you again," he said.

Maggie jerked to attention. He stood beside her table. "Hi," she said.

"How's the research coming?"

"G-g-g." Why couldn't she get any words out? She nodded instead.

"Rachel said you were the social media specialist for the magazine. Multi-tasking with the research? The two jobs don't sound related, but I suppose in this day and age, businesses want the most bang for their employee buck, huh?"

"Part of my job," she managed to say. "Promotion for the magazine." There. That wasn't so hard.

He nodded. "I see. Any luck finding a place to live?"

Maggie sighed. No secrets in a small town. "I'm still l-l-l." She slapped her thigh to break the word free, but it wasn't coming. "Not yet."

Thad narrowed his eyes as if to assess her. If he hadn't noticed the stutter before, no way he could have missed it now. "Enjoy your day."

And that was that. Just as well. Once he discovered she was writing about his fascination for Virginia Carter, any attempts he made at polite conversation would likely end.

Maybe he wouldn't find out about her blog posts. Men didn't generally subscribe to *Reading Women.*

"Well, look who else found this hole in the wall." Preston's voice made her cringe like a bite of too-sweet lemon bars.

Maggie shaded her eyes with one hand, hoping to avoid a confrontation.

"So what brings you here? W-w-working?" Preston asked with a snicker.

Maggie shut down her computer and tucked it into her bag, refusing to engage.

"What's the m-m-matter?" Preston went on. "C-c-cat got your t-t-tongue?

She shouldered past him to leave the café, Preston's laughter following her.

Once she'd reached the sidewalk, a hand settled on her shoulder. Maggie shrugged away and rounded on whoever thought it was okay to touch her. "What?"

"You okay?" Thad Benson asked.

Oh no, she was not giving this man knight in shining armor status.

"He likes to make fun of the way I t-t-t..." Maggie shook her head, embarrassed by her difficulty forming a clean sentence. "Speak."

"Why put up with it? Doesn't your silence give him what he wants? Or walking out?"

"You have no idea..." she began, enunciating every word. She lowered her voice. "If I engage him, as you suggest, and if I stutter, he gleefully pounces on every word and exacerbates the problem. If I refuse to engage, I shut him down." She blinked, amazed she'd spoken without a hitch.

Thad graced her with one of his smiles, the distracting crease in his cheek giving him a roguish sort of charm. "Not very gentlemanly. I'd be happy to punch the guy's lights out for you. If you want," he said.

A do-gooder, then, one she couldn't take her eyes off. His features were so distinctive. "Thank you, but don't bother. He's not worth the effort." Her pulse raced, imagining her knight doing battle for her. Heat rose to her cheeks. "Can I buy you dinner tonight?" she asked before she had time to consider her words.

He stared at her a moment, causing her to look away. Dumb move.

"To thank you," she added quickly. "I realize you're probably married. I did see you carrying diapers." Maggie smiled sheepishly. "Your wife could join us." She needed to stop talking.

"I'm not married. The diapers were for my nephew, but I think I'll pass, just the same. Don't take it personal."

40

No, she didn't take it personally. She already knew he preferred his fantasy world with Virginia to a warm-blooded woman. What a waste. The man oozed testosterone. She might have played the new-in-town-and-looking-for-information card, an innocent invitation, but that would be a lie. Thad Benson disrupted her insides like a cat pouncing on a birdbath, causing all kinds of flutters.

Thad wasn't the only one living a rich fantasy life.

Chapter 6

A my leaned against the door between the showroom and the shop, arms folded while Thad peeled the stencil off Old Man Sims' headstone. He could guess she had something on her mind, but he wasn't going to encourage her. Not today. He had enough things to think about.

Starting with Maggie Grant. He still wanted to flatten the guy who'd made fun of her stutter.

Amy crossed the shop and traced a finger along the lines of the dog Thad had hand-carved above the sandblasted name and dates.

"You're really good, you know," she said.

So this was about the sculpting again. Thad wasn't in the mood. He continued to work in silence.

"You going to the next Cemetery Association meeting?" she asked.

"Yes."

"You could offer to do a demonstration."

Thad straightened and gave her a deliberate look. "Funny, Garth said the same thing. I don't suppose the two of you are ganging up on me, are you?"

Amy grinned. "If you won't listen to one of us, maybe you'll listen to the other."

"Look." He reached for a towel to wipe his hands. "The last Cemetery Association meeting I went to, I got the 'intruder' stare from all the old timers. I'm not Dad, and they want to make sure I know it. Like I told Garth, I'm not much of a show-off, and those guys already don't want to give me the time of day."

"Another reason to do the demonstration. Interact with them. Show them you've got the goods. If you sit quietly in the corner, the funeral directors will send their work elsewhere, over to Foxfield or the assembly-line shops. You need to show that you offer something more, something different." She nodded to the scrap corner. "All those garden statues tell me that's the part of the job you like. You don't have orders for all of them. Pursue your passion, Thad."

"It's a hobby. Something to fill the time."

"A hobby you can turn into cash flow," she said. "Bring those statues into the office space where people can see them. Put them on the front lawn outside the store to pull people in."

Was she trying to tell him, in her not-so-subtle way, the business was in worse shape than he thought? "Are we having a cash flow problem that I don't know about?"

Amy didn't answer immediately. "Not necessarily cash flow, but you and Brian and I won't be getting a raise this year, and it's a good thing Garth isn't officially on the payroll anymore."

Thad glanced at the statues and ornaments he'd carved from the scraps, essentially throw-away material. If some sucker wanted to buy them, he could at least give his siblings bonuses, even if he couldn't give them raises.

"Nothing to lose in putting them out, is there?" she asked.

"I guess. But don't expect everyone else to share your opinion of my hobby." She had a tendency to be more of a meddler when her husband was traveling. "When is Kevin getting back from his press conference?"

"Ohh!" she said, rubbing her hands together. "Kevin could do a write-up in his column, the same way he wrote about my epitaphs when we first met. I bet you'd have orders to keep you busy all day, every day."

"You're nuts. Nobody wants my garbage."

Amy grabbed him by the collar, pulling him to face level. "None of us wants to see the business fail, Thaddeus Benson. You're missing your niche. I have mine. Garth found his. Why can't you believe your own eyes? You have a gift." She released him with a jerk.

He chuckled. "And to think, we were always worried you couldn't take care of yourself. Look at you now."

She spun toward the showroom. "I'm getting my camera and I'm going to take pictures. You need a catalog. A portfolio. Where's Brian? I need him to haul this stuff to the front lawn."

Thad shot a glance at the clock on the wall. He needed to disappear while Amy was ordering people around, before she concocted more schemes. He slipped out the back door of the shop and headed for the cemetery park and fresh air to clear his thoughts.

He passed a graveside service in the new section and continued to the angel markers on the hill, past Owen Matthews' obelisk. He slowed, turned and took a second look at the graveside service. Benson Monuments hadn't gotten the stone order. Of course, they weren't the only game in town, but since his father had retired, Thad noticed more new graves he hadn't received orders for. The Cemetery Association already viewed him as the newcomer, despite the long family history. He had to prove himself to get recommendations. Amy might have a point. Showing off his craft might not be a bad idea.

Thad stopped beside Ginny's stone. Twice in one week. Back in the day, he talked to her more than about anyone else. She might not be able to offer her opinions anymore, but he found peace beside her grave, sharing confidences he didn't feel comfortable telling anyone else. The best part being he knew whatever he said wouldn't go any further. Dead men—or, in this case, women—tell no tales.

"What do you think?" he said, taking a seat on the grass in front of the stone. "Are they right? Who am I to argue if some dumb schmuck wants to buy a piece of scrap? If it brings in more money for the monument shop, why not?"

Amy might be able to hear the dead, but none of the rest of them had "the gift." In truth, he didn't want answers, even from Ginny. If she were sitting here now, she'd probably ask him what the big deal was. What was the worst that could happen?

He didn't like putting himself out there. Thad had seen too many bullies, too many mean people. He preferred his own company, or that of his family. Whenever he came across someone worth talking to in this world, they were counterbalanced with people like that asshole in the café this morning, the one who'd pointed out Maggie's stutter. Who would make fun of another's person's difficulties?

Thad closed his eyes to let the breeze sweep over him, the closest he came to physical touch these days.

And he thought of Maggie, the woman who'd invited him to dinner.

His fingers tingled. He had a new face to commit to stone. No, he wasn't the dating type, but he could express his appreciation for Maggie Grant the only way he knew how.

Chapter 7

When Maggie let herself in the front door of Torie's townhouse, her sister met her, arms outstretched.

"There she is," Torie said.

Maggie set her tote bag down and hugged her sister tight. "So good to see you."

Torie backed away and pointed a finger at her. "If you still lived here, you could see me every day."

Maggie pointed back. "We've been over this."

"If it's about the money…"

"It isn't just about the money," Maggie said. Even if money did play a role.

She reached into her bag and retrieved her notebook and her copy of the book they'd agreed to read.

"I'm warming taco dip. Can you put out the wine glasses?" Torie asked, disappearing into the kitchen.

"Got it." Maggie set five glasses on the dining room table, found a bowl and emptied a bag of chips into it.

"Hey, before I forget," Torie said, oven mitts on her hands as she carried the dip. "Mom called a little while ago. She was going to call you, but I told her I'd relay the information since we were getting together tonight. Lacey's flying in from California with her

47

latest boyfriend for the Fourth of July. Mom's hoping we can all get together."

"Did she check with Lacey on everyone getting together?" Maggie asked with a healthy dose of skepticism.

Torie set her dish on a hot pad and slipped the oven mitts off. "Surely she'll expect it. Rumor has it this guy has the potential to be husband number two."

"Then she definitely won't want me there. She still blames me for losing husband number one, despite the issues they had before he met me." Maggie set her hands on her hips. "How bad is it when my own sister's husband has to defend my disorder?"

"You hardly stutter anymore." Torie gave Maggie a hug. "Lacey's matured since she's moved out west."

"If the first thirty years didn't do it, not sure how the last five would make much difference." Maggie sighed. "I'll go. For Mom's sake."

"Hello?" Jean called from the front door.

"Well, come in," Torie said.

Maggie glanced out the window. Blanca was getting out of her car on the street, but she couldn't see Edie's car yet.

A moment later, Blanca walked in. She took a look around and grinned. "You are too organized, Maggie," she said, nodding at Maggie's notebook. "You make me feel like such a slacker."

"I read too many books over the course of a month to keep them all straight," Maggie replied. "I *need* those notes to remember which one is which."

"Are the other ladies coming?" Jean asked. "Your new friends?"

"Not this time," Maggie said. "Not enough notice to find babysitters. Both of them were worried three kids would overwhelm the menfolk, but they'll make arrangements so they can come next time."

"New blood?" Blanca asked.

"Do you mind?" Maggie replied.

"Always room for a couple more. Make sure they know to bring a bottle of wine."

Jean chuckled.

"So what did you all think of the book?" Maggie asked, taking a seat at the dining room table.

Blanca and Jean exchanged glances. Before they could answer, Edie knocked on the door and let herself in.

"How about a glass of that aforementioned wine?" Torie asked.

Blanca took a glass from the table. "Thought you'd never ask."

Maggie glanced at each of them. "Someone read the book other than me, didn't they?"

"Wine for me, too," Jean said.

"I read it," Edie said. "But I can't say I enjoyed it. Took me all damn month."

"DNF for me," Jean said, with a pout Maggie's direction. "Sorry, Mags."

"I'm still trying, but it's a chore," Blanca said.

Torie returned with a bottle and poured a glass for everyone. "Fine. That's the last time I make a group recommendation. It's still a good excuse to get together, don't you think?"

Maggie tossed her notebook toward her tote bag. "Guess I won't be needing any notes, then. She held a glass out for her sister.

The evening devolved from there with Blanca telling the group about her husband's recent vasectomy and how she wasn't going near him until he was proclaimed sperm free. Edie asked where she was going for sex in the interim and received a glare in return. Jean complained about her lack of a love life and pointed out the Haunted Heathcliff blog (since Amy and Sandra hadn't come) which prompted the group to pry more information from Maggie. She refused to elaborate and all eyes turned to Torie, who remained suspiciously quiet. Edie and Blanca eventually coaxed Torie to tell all about her latest boyfriend, the one Maggie thought might stick—if Maggie got out of the way long enough.

A couple of hours and several bottles of wine later, book club disbanded and Maggie retreated to her old bedroom, not sober enough to drive. She changed into her pajamas, did her evening bathroom routine and stuck her head into Torie's room to say goodnight.

Torie sat on her bed, smiling, whispering into her phone.

She wouldn't need to whisper if Maggie wasn't there, and there was a better than even chance the phone call would be an in-person conversation without a big sister in the way.

Torie sprang to her feet. "Hold on a sec," she said. "Everything okay?" she asked Maggie.

"Wanted to say goodnight. I'll probably be gone before you get up in the morning."

Torie gave her a hug. "If you want to talk some more…"

Maggie shook her head. "Wiped out. And you'd only try to convince me to stay again. I have my own life to get on with, you know."

How many years had her little sister spent trying to take care of Maggie? It might have begun when Torie started earning a bigger paycheck, but Maggie could backtrack further, to high school and the kids who'd made fun of Maggie's speech. Torie had always been a fierce defender, unlike their little sister, Lacey.

"You know, if you want to schedule a rendezvous with whoever's on the other end of that phone call, you don't have to stick around on my account," Maggie said.

Torie frowned, touches of pink coloring her cheeks. "And where else would I go?"

They both knew the answer. Maggie raised her eyebrows and Torie returned the expression, daring her to voice her thoughts. Torie tilted the phone to her ear. "I gotta go. I'll talk to you later."

"You didn't have to hang up on him," Maggie said.

"He'll be there tomorrow. You, on the other hand, are going to abandon me again." Torie took Maggie's hands. "You okay?"

"Couldn't be better. Please don't worry about me. I hate to see you missing out…"

"We've been over this." Torie tugged her to sit on the bed. "Tell me about Haunted Heathcliff. Jean seems to think you've developed a crush on this guy."

Most likely it was her Heathcliff attribution that stoked her imagination. "Just a guy in the cemetery." A guy who reminded her how long she'd been without a man.

51

"And you want to help him forget this dead girl who continues to haunt him? Be the one who reminds him there is a vibrant woman standing in front of him?"

Maggie laughed. If it helped Torie move on in her relationship… "He has possibilities, as long as my little sister doesn't get in the way."

Torie gave her a playful shove. "Go to bed."

"Thanks for letting me stay."

"Still your house, too," Torie said wistfully.

Maggie reached for Torie's hand. "I miss you, too."

Upon her return to Edgarville the next morning, Maggie dropped her bag at the rental, looked around, and decided the weather was too nice to stay indoors. She shoved her current reading assignment into her purse and walked to the cemetery. Definitely not because she wanted to see Thad Benson again.

Okay, maybe a little.

Maggie had a ringside seat to Virginia Carter's headstone, so she was right there when Thad appeared a couple hours later. Like he did the last time Maggie had seen him there, Thad kissed his fingers and touched the top of the stone. Like the last time, her heart ached for him.

He stretched, glanced around the cemetery, and locked his gaze with Maggie's. Thad Benson definitely had a romantic hero aura to him, even more so after he'd offered to defend Maggie against that jackhole, Preston Andrews.

Thad didn't move for a minute. When he did, he headed her direction.

Maggie's heart skipped a beat. Caught.

"We meet again," he said, stopping well out of socially accepted conversation range.

She nodded, those birds fluttering inside her again. He wasn't interested in a date, or anything else. He'd already made that clear. Try to explain that to her too-long-without-a-man hormones, to her Heathcliff fantasies.

"What brings you out here today?" he asked.

"Good place to read," she said, omitting the part where she'd hoped to see him again.

"About dinner," he said, his deep voice rumbling across her skin. "I've never had a woman offer to buy me dinner before. In my world, that's the gentleman's responsibility."

Maggie put a hand to her heart. Was he going to ask her out?

"Even when it's two friends sharing a meal." He studied his hands a moment, then snuck a glance at her. "I'd like to buy you dinner to apologize for my rude behavior."

Okay, expectations set, even if she chose to read more into it than he was offering. "I can do that." *Liar.*

He took a step closer. "There's an Italian restaurant on the other end of Main Street. Riccardo's."

Skip the restaurant. Maggie envisioned Heathcliff and Catherine running to each other across the moor, embracing, releasing their passion for each other.

Except she wasn't Catherine. Virginia Carter was, apparently. Imagination check.

"When?"

"Five o'clock? That'll give me time to go home and get cleaned up." He brushed at his work pants and a cloud of dust rose in the breeze.

"Meet you there?" she said.

He smiled, tipped two fingers to his forehead and headed down the hill.

Maggie nearly collapsed on the bench. She closed her eyes, still feeling his voice all over her body.

Friends. He'd said two friends sharing a meal. Friends might share a friendly kiss goodnight at the end of the evening, wouldn't they? What if she offered the "no strings attached" package? Would he go for a one-night offer?

She shook her head. Yes, he was all man, but that didn't give her the right to objectify him. Thad Benson was a do-gooder, which meant he would also be a perfect gentleman. She'd be lucky if he'd offer—or accept—an innocent—or not so innocent—goodnight kiss.

Which didn't stop her from wanting one.

Maggie returned to her computer and wrote the next installment of her blog, impressions of a man who reined in his desires for fear of being disloyal to his dead girlfriend. Haunted by memories of her. A noble knight, doomed to an existence of self-imposed celibacy.

Maggie spent the rest of the day reading one of her book assignments. She took the time to do her make-up and hair, and donned a summery dress and heeled sandals. No one said friends shouldn't look good, although she'd managed her expectations about a kiss. For all she knew, this was a pity date, one where Mr. Do-Gooder was putting on his Mountie hat and giving the poor, stuttering girl a night on the town because, lord knows, stuttering girls couldn't find a date on their own. No thank you. She'd had her share of those kinds of dates.

On the other hand, she might be able to manipulate him into a kiss, or something more. If he wanted to feel sorry for her, might as well find out how sorry for her he was.

Maggie laughed at her out-of-control thoughts. Mr. Do-Gooder wasn't likely to offer himself as a pity prize. As a "perfect gentlemen," he wouldn't want to take advantage of a lady, even if the lady wanted him to. He'd already played the friend card—a clear message.

Maggie walked from her rental to the Italian restaurant. Riccardo's was on the end of Main Street, the way Thad had said. Inside, she approached the hostess stand. "I'm meeting a friend. Thad Benson."

"Right this way," the hostess said. "Follow me."

He'd already arrived? She glanced around.

Maggie trailed the woman to a booth where Thad sat, his back to her.

"Your server will be with you in a minute," the hostess said.

Thad turned and rose to his feet. More of that gentleman stuff. He'd shaved and changed into a pair of jeans and a button-down shirt.

Maggie smiled and took her seat on the bench opposite him, but he didn't resume his seat immediately. And he was staring at her.

"Is something wrong?" she asked quietly.

"Wow."

Yes, she'd been fantasizing about Thad, but the intensity of his scrutiny, the way his eyes scanned every inch of her face, reminded her she was too chicken to act on said fantasies. The birds in her chest were fluttering again. She tilted her head, waiting for him to elaborate.

Thad slid into his seat, his face taking on a ruddy hue. "You look nice," he said. "Not that you didn't look nice before, but you look different in a dress." He rubbed a hand over his face. "Now you know why I don't date. Not exactly the smooth type. I get a little tongue-tied."

His way of acknowledging her stutter? He'd noticed the effort she'd made with her appearance, though. *Note to self, wear more dresses.* "Then it's a good thing we're just friends," she said. "If it helps to know, your nerves make me more at ease, less tongue-tied."

"I didn't mean... I wasn't referring to..."

Maggie smiled. "I know I stutter. It's okay."

"Help a guy out. Tell me what a dork I am. Or as my sister likes to tell me, I'm a troglodyte. Better yet, tell me what prompted you to ask me to dinner in the first place."

"I already told you—to thank you," she said. "For offering to beat up the bully. I'd probably let you if we were still in high school." She wasn't about to tell him how attracted she'd been to him, how attracted she still was, but his awkwardness removed some of the tragic hero attributes she'd bestowed on him. Thad wasn't a brooder the way Heathcliff was.

"Ah, the troglodyte in me. Some things a guy never quite grows out of."

"I'm guessing troglodyte is a term of endearment," she said.

56

He smiled, crinkling that crease in his cheek and the lines around his eyes. Thad wasn't handsome in the traditional sense of the word, but he had an interesting face, expressive and filled with character.

"My brothers and I might have been a little overprotective of our little sister when she was growing up. She…" He hesitated, considered his words. "She didn't always fit in."

Like Maggie hadn't fit in. "Have you considered that was because she had a band of brothers following her around?" she teased.

His expression went serious, as if he hadn't considered the possibility before. He relaxed again. "No, but it probably didn't help. You sound like the voice of experience. You have brothers?"

Maggie shook her head. "No, just sisters. Two, one of whom was constantly embarrassed by me."

"Why? Because of your speech?" he asked.

"Yeah."

"You've hardly stuttered once since we've been here. How does that work?"

"I'm what you call a covert stutterer. I tend to avoid words that might trip me up and, for the most part, my stuttering has resolved itself, even if, as you've seen, I still stumble from time to time. Lots of years with speech pathologists. But don't ask me to phone in an order for a pizza."

He laughed. "Really?"

She shrugged. "For whatever reason, talking on the phone can be difficult."

"My offer to punch that guy in the café still stands."

"Defender of the weak," Maggie said with a smile. "I'm not weak, for the record, and as I mentioned previously, he isn't worth the effort."

"I suppose you're right."

A waitress appeared beside their table. "You two ready to order?"

"Oh!" Maggie checked her menu. "I'm sorry. I haven't even looked yet. Give us a minute?"

The waitress gave her an odd look and walked away.

"Now I'm feeling self-conscious," she told Thad. "First you, now the waitress. Do I have a pimple breaking out or something?"

Thad glanced after the waitress. "More likely she's pegged you as a new face, coupled with the fact you're having dinner with Edgarville's confirmed bachelor."

Maggie set her menu down. Here was her opening to find out more about his relationship with Virginia Carter. "What makes you a confirmed bachelor?"

He held her gaze a moment—a very intense moment that sent shivers up her arms—before he answered. "I like it that way."

And he was right back to Heathcliff status.

Chapter 8

The more Maggie talked, the more Thad was convinced he'd chosen the right subject for his first attempt at a full-size statue.

She ate her lasagna as she chattered, filling in for his lack of small talk. He was impressed with the way she acknowledged her stutter with humor and acceptance, admitting how people made fun of her, something she'd endured and survived, making her stronger in the process.

Like Amy, Maggie faced extraordinary challenges growing up. For Amy, it had been her gift with epitaphs. For Maggie, it was her speech.

Maggie described one of her sisters as her fiercest defender, and while she didn't say much about the other sister, he got the impression there was something awkward there.

Even as she joked about her experiences, the obstacles she'd overcome, Thad ached to take on the bullies in her past—including the one sister—and make them apologize.

When dessert arrived, she took a bite of her cannoli, closed her eyes and hummed her pleasure—a hum that went straight to his groin. Not a big brother response.

Despite Maggie's healthy appetite, the contours of her arms showed efficient muscle "engines" to burn off any excess calories. Her bone structure was exquisite. Thad tried to commit every detail of her physique to memory.

No, he wasn't Michelangelo, but he had an eye for beauty. Maggie's distinctive features set her apart from the crowd, features he wanted to look at every night. As much as he was enjoying their dinner, their conversation, he was eager to get home and mold a clay model of Maggie Grant.

"You're staring," she said.

He knew he was. "I didn't mean to be rude," he said. "But I will admit I'm enjoying your appreciation for your food." She had made a show of it, after all, and that sounded better than telling her he wanted to touch her arms—and other parts of her body—to replicate in stone.

Her tongue darted out to wet her lips, and her eyes shimmered. It had been a long time since he'd been so aware of a woman, but experience told him he was better keeping his hands to himself. Aside from Ginny, relationships tended to go downhill after the clothes came off. Ginny was the only woman he'd slept with who appreciated sex as a recreational sport and not a lifelong commitment. No, he was happier without the expectations or the awkwardness.

Thad signed the check, cleared his throat and backed away from the table. "Thanks for joining me for dinner. Always nice to make new friends. You'll let me know if I can do anything for you while you're finding your way around town?"

She nodded, a sign she was nervous? Maggie hadn't stuttered more than once or twice all through dinner, but he'd come to recognize the head bob as a way to avoid speaking. He helped her with her chair and stood aside to follow her out.

When they reached the sidewalk, she turned, an expectant look in her eye. Her chest rose and fell with a deep breath.

"Thank you for dinner," she said in that sultry voice.

"My pleasure."

"Gentleman or not, next time it's my treat. That's what friends do, after all."

Check. She'd gotten the friend message, something he was reconsidering with the way her voice stroked him. He was tempted to suggest other benefits to being friends.

"Okay," she said. "This is awkward. For the record, I do hug my friends when we part. Do you mind?"

He glanced over his shoulder, at the people inside the restaurant who were probably watching. He could expect to be teased as a result of having dinner with a woman, and he didn't want to make things worse. With a nod to the side of the building, he guided her out of public view, to the alley beside the restaurant.

Maggie stepped into his embrace, and as her breasts pressed against his chest, he sprang to life once more. Her warm skin smelled like flowers, and without thinking, he molded his hands to her arms, tracing the musculature. He continued his exploration along the contours of her back, closed his eyes and cupped her bottom, measuring the curves.

Her voice was whisper soft against his neck. "Do you hug everyone this way?"

He pulled away, suddenly aware he'd touched her inappropriately.

Maggie tipped to her toes and touched her lips to his. "Maybe not just friends," she said, her voice sliding over him like silk. She lowered, let her hand fall to his waist, trailing across his butt, and then she gave him a finger wave as she headed down the sidewalk.

Damn. It was going to take him a minute to step out from between the buildings and not embarrass himself.

Thad wasn't sure what to make of Maggie. The kiss, while innocent on the surface, had his blood racing. He shouldn't have touched her the way he had, but in his hands, he'd imagined a piece of marble, smooth and silky.

She was a lot warmer than a piece of marble.

He wasn't going to make more of this than there was. She hadn't thrown herself at him. She hadn't suggested taking him home, or having him take her home. Was she going to expect him to call her?

He sucked at the whole man-woman thing. This was why he preferred to remain a bachelor. Yes, intimate female companionship might be nice once in a while, but he'd been burned too many times.

Thad marched to his car and climbed in. He played the steering wheel like a drum set on the drive home, more agitated than he'd been in months—no, years. Because of an innocent kiss?

No, it had been more than a kiss. She'd asked for a hug and he'd practically groped her in the alley beside the restaurant. This was on him.

He arrived in his garage, turned off the car and bypassed the house. He headed straight for his workshop in the backyard, pulled out his keys and inserted one into the lock. A sense of calm descended on him when he flipped on the lights.

Faces looked back at him—Ginny, carved into a piece of stone. A bust of Helena, the nurse he'd met at the hospital after Ginny died. A relief of Danae.

Danae. He'd liked her—a lot—but she'd left him to marry someone else.

And finally, an abandoned mold he'd done of another woman who'd turned out to be less attractive on the inside.

Did he know enough about Maggie to sculpt her?

Yes. His dating days might be over, but he could still appreciate an interesting face. And body. This one would be more than a portrait, more than a bust. Thad wanted to portray all of Maggie. He'd held her in his arms, felt the sinews. The softness.

The heat.

He wouldn't be able to shake off her effect on him until he'd cast her in stone.

Thad pulled out a glob of modeling clay and set to work, massaging a miniature of Maggie's startling eyes, caressing her cheekbones, the oval of her face, the texture of her curls. He rolled a second chunk of clay between his hands and started on her core, sculpting the athletic build of her arms, the gentle curve of her breasts, narrowing to her waist and the slope of her back. He closed his eyes, remembering her round bottom.

Not a nude. He'd sculpt her in the dress. Sitting.

With another clump of clay, he added the skirt, working his way up to carve the bodice with a thumb.

He set the model on his workbench. How long had it been since he'd slept with a woman? Thad glanced at Danae's face, raised against the stone background.

He might have married Danae. If he'd proposed, would she have left him for that other guy? In retrospect, she'd become distant long before that. Disconnected. If he was honest, he was more in love with the carving he'd done of her than the woman it represented. She did have a beautiful face, but in the end, she'd told him making headstones was a spooky job. Truth? Or a convenient excuse?

All the women he'd dated told him his job made them uncomfortable. Cemeteries were filled with ghosts and ghouls and scary things that go bump in the night.

Maggie didn't seem uncomfortable in the cemetery. She'd chosen to work there.

His eyes drifted to the figure he'd modeled, still crude, but all Maggie.

The chances of things going any further between them were remote, at best, but he could hold onto her in spirit, remember her face, and with a full sculpture, remember the rest of her, as well.

Thad rubbed his eyes with the backs of his hands and glanced at the window. Daylight glowed around the edges of the blinds. How long had it been since he'd worked on something all night?

Maggie was an interesting subject. He'd order a piece of marble—the cost would set him back, but a sculpture of Maggie would be worth it—so he could get started right away.

With one last caress to the chin of his model, he left the workshop. He'd likely be useless for the rest of the day, but he had a business to run—or run into the ground.

Chapter 9

After finishing the next installment of her so-called Haunted Heathcliff blog, Maggie checked the internet connection in her rental. Nothing. She set her phone on the table to use as a hot spot, but cell coverage was spotty on a good day, and it wasn't cooperating now. She had to transmit her work to the magazine.

Maggie carried her phone to the patio doors. Even if she found a connection, she wasn't sure it would stay connected.

The café had Wi-Fi. And tea. And fresh pastries.

She packed her computer, grabbed her purse and keys from the countertop. The mirror beside the door stopped her.

Looking herself in the eye, she questioned her assignment for the umpteenth time. Three days ago, Thad had been a grieving stranger. He was no longer a stranger—well, less of a stranger. A pang of guilt told her she was exploiting him. What would he think if he read the blog? She hadn't identified him by name, but he would certainly recognize himself, even though no one else had.

Their duck into the alley last night for an innocent hug demonstrated to Maggie that he was a private person, and here she was, displaying his grief to the world, or at least the segment of the world who read her blog.

Innocent hug. Hah! She'd exploited that, too. Once he'd allowed her "in," she'd gone all in. Granted, it could have been construed as an innocent kiss, but on her end, it had been an invitation. He hadn't accepted, in spite of his obvious physical response. And what did Maggie do? She'd turned his decision not to pursue more of a kiss, not to explain his roving hands, into another Heathcliff blog post.

He hadn't accepted anything from her. Thad had made it clear he wasn't the dating type, that it was a friendly dinner. Maggie was the one who hadn't respected his clearly set boundaries. Well, sort of. After skirting those boundaries, she likely wouldn't get another dinner invitation—or anything else, for that matter.

The blog wasn't a betrayal of their friendship. It was mostly fiction, enhanced by the influences of Emily Brontë. Friendship? More of an acquaintance. Maggie gave her reflection a nod and left the apartment for the café.

Sunlight filtered through mature oaks and Japanese lilacs and linden trees. Not a whisper of wind on a cool summer morning. Since she was going to be on Main Street, she could stop in the real estate office after she posted her blog for Sloane's review and get started on finding a place to live, a place with a more reliable internet connection.

With a renewed attitude, she walked into the café and headed for the counter with a smile. "Good morning. Blueberry tea and an apple turnover, please."

Sandra wiped her hands on a towel before she rang up the sale, eyeing Maggie speculatively. "Good morning to you."

Maggie used her phone to pay for her snack while Sandra filled the order.

"Heard you had dinner with Thad last night," Sandra said.

Maggie froze, her hand hovering over the tray. "How…?" But she knew the answer. Small town. Not to mention Sandra was Thad's sister-in-law.

And the web of deception grew larger. These folks would run her out of town when they discovered who her mystery man at the cemetery was.

Sandra grinned. "Don't worry, nobody's reading anything into it, but it did raise some eyebrows. Thad keeps to himself most of the time. He's friendly enough, but when he's here, or over at the bar, he's like a surveillance camera. Silent. Watching, but you know he's there. Know what I mean?"

"I do."

"I didn't mean to upset you," Sandra said, "but I thought you should know the word's out and people are curious."

"He offered to defend me against my nemesis at the m-m-magazine and I wanted to thank him."

"That's our Thad." Sandra reached for Maggie's hands, squeezed, then took the tray and carried it to a table for her. She glanced around the café, waited for Maggie to sit and then sat with her.

"The three of them—Thad and Garth and Brian— they've always been like bodyguards for Amy. People gave her a hard time in school, and I'm ashamed to admit I was one of those mean girls. As far as I know,

Amy didn't have a real date until she met Kevin, and even then, her brothers tried their best to intimidate him. They all have a protective streak a mile wide. They seem a little lost since she got married, although they do have the little ones to hover over now. Except Brian. He's… umm… I'll call it distracted by one of the barmaids over at Murphy's. She's currently leading him around by the… by the nose." Sandra winked. "If you know what I mean."

"I'm getting an idea, yes." Maggie didn't meet Sandra's eye. The more she heard, the guiltier she felt, but she had a job to do. Bills to pay. A house to buy. Or not, if she was going to lose her job. Sloane had been unpredictable after the move.

"But Thad," Sandra continued. "He's a tough nut. Hard to get to know." She leaned over the table and lowered her voice. "Garth called me this morning from the monument shop. He said Thad looks like he hasn't been to bed."

Maggie straightened in her chair and folded her hands in her lap. Was Sandra asking if they'd slept together? If Maggie was the reason Thad looked haggard this morning? Maggie's definition of 'friend' was growing more rigid.

"Is it customary for him to stay up all night?" Maggie asked, her words enunciated and as crisp as she could make them.

Sandra laughed. "I didn't mean to imply…" She laughed again. "I'm sorry. Of course you would have thought I was prying after I said such an indelicate thing about Brian. I didn't mean to imply you'd spent the night together. No, as someone Thad has accepted into his circle of friends, I thought you might know what was bothering him."

Maggie blinked several times, not sure what to think. She released a pent-up breath. "As you said, he's a hard man to know. We had a pleasant dinner and then we each went to our own homes. I don't even know where he lives. I hardly consider myself a friend."

Sandra patted Maggie's hands and rose from her seat. "He doesn't have dinner with just anyone. You are definitely on his friend list." She cocked her head. "Maybe he didn't make *your* list. I shouldn't assume... but I've never known Thad to offend anyone without cause."

Maggie forced a smile. "He didn't offend me. It was an innocent dinner, but I'd be surprised if there was a repeat."

"That would be a shame," Sandra said. "I thought the two of you..." She shrugged. "Can't blame a girl for trying." She returned to the counter to greet a customer.

Sandra wasn't the only one who'd hoped Thad might be interested in a mutually beneficial friendship. All else aside, the blog would probably put an end to that once he found out.

Maggie started her computer, took a bite of her turnover, and sent the post, but Sandra's words nagged her.

With her mission accomplished and Sandra's customer gone, Maggie waved Sandra to the table. If she wanted to find out more about Virginia Carter and Thad Benson, Sandra seemed like someone who would know.

"What can I do for you?" Sandra asked. "More tea?"

"Something's bothering me. The dots don't connect," she said. "You mentioned the whole town knew I had dinner with Thad last night…"

"Well, maybe not the whole town…"

"And then you said your husband didn't think Thad had slept last night, but you didn't believe it was because he and I…" Maggie waved a hand in the air between her and the absent man in question. "You've piqued my curiosity. Is there something I don't know about Thad? Is there a woman in his past who's soured him for the rest of womankind? A dead wife? A manipulative girlfriend? Or is it me?"

"Oh, oh, oh." Sandra raised her hands. "I didn't mean anything… Oh, Maggie, no. It isn't anything like that. It's just that Thad, well, he's not a very social guy. It must be years since I've seen him on an honest-to-god date. I think he prefers his solitude. No dead wife. No awful girlfriend that I'm aware of." She gave a nervous laugh. "See what happens when you talk too much? It's definitely not a reflection on you. Please don't think that."

Except she did. Maggie had fallen into the old trap of being "less than perfect," which had started her thinking down that avenue.

The relationship between Thad and Virginia Carter was either too long ago, or Thad had kept Virginia a close secret.

What other secrets was he keeping?

Chapter 10

Thad wiped his brow with a bandana while Brian put the last of his tools into the toolbox in the bed of the pickup truck. Garth peeled off his gloves and the three of them took one last look at Old Man Sims's headstone.

Gathering clouds signaled a thunderstorm in the not-too-distant future. Thad welcomed the break in the oppressive humidity.

"What do you say we head to Murphy's?" he said. "I'll buy."

"Not going to say no to a free beer," Garth said, tucking his gloves into his pocket.

"I'm in," Brian replied.

They climbed into the truck and Thad drove the couple of blocks to Main Street.

When they walked into the bar, Patrick waved to them, an indication he'd start their drink order. Delia carried her tray to the pass to wait. She didn't, however, rush to greet Brian, an oversight Brian hurried to remedy. The poor girl gave him a weary smile as he approached and she offered him a cheek. Thad would lay odds a break-up was in Brian's future. Brian couldn't continue to hover over her the way he did, certainly cutting into her tips while he tried to mark his territory like a dog.

There wasn't a man in Edgarville who didn't know Brian was dating Delia. Brian, however, was the only man in Edgarville who didn't seem to understand she wasn't looking for an exclusive relationship. Flirting meant better tips, or at least that's what she'd told him, but he had a definite jealous streak.

"How much longer you think she'll put up with him?" Garth said as he and Thad took their seats.

"I was thinking the same thing. I'll give it two weeks," Thad said.

"With the look on her face? Can you see her? I won't give him past the weekend, and that's being generous."

Thad chuckled. "It's her own fault. She's the one who thought it would be fun to rattle his cage."

She carried the tray to their table with Brian in tow. Brian was making a nuisance of himself, telling her which men in the bar were eyeing her and to watch out for them. To her credit, she didn't respond, merely raised her eyebrows at him.

Poor sap didn't realize he was helping her choose her next fling.

Brian took his seat at the table while Delia set their drinks in front of them. His eyes were fixed on her as she sashayed to the bar.

"She's pretty, don't you think?" Brian asked, taking a gulp of his beer.

He said the same thing every time. Thad and Garth exchanged glances.

"Definitely thick in the head," Garth said to Thad.

"Without a doubt," Thad replied.

Brian scowled. "Hey. I'm not so dumb."

"Sometimes…" Garth said, swallowing a drink with an exaggerated "Ahhh."

Brian inclined toward Thad. "So what's the deal with the new girl in town? Heard you took her to dinner."

Thad shot Brian a 'don't go there' look but, honestly, sometimes his brother was dumber than a rock.

Garth's mouth twisted with a grin. "According to Sandra, Sir Galahad here offered to take care of someone who made fun of her, and Maggie—that's her name, in case you wanted to know—invited him to dinner."

Thad narrowed his eyes and lifted his mug, not bothering to confirm or deny. His personal life was none of their business.

"Joke's on her," Brian said, tipping his chair backward. "Been so long since he's been on a date, he probably doesn't know what to do with a woman anymore."

Thad stretched his legs out under the table and hooked one of the legs of Brian's chair. Brian jumped to his feet as his chair went to the floor. The idiot never learned.

Garth tilted his head back and roared with laughter, wiping at his eyes.

A hand rested on Thad's shoulder and he looked up. Rachel Morrison, and her eyes were red. He rose to his feet. "What's wrong?"

"Could you…" She cleared her throat and her eyes welled with tears. She glanced at Garth. "Both of you." Her voice was thick with emotion. "My Beau crossed the rainbow bridge this morning." She paused to blow her nose. "Garth, you did such a lovely plaque for the Callahans when their dog passed, I thought…"

Thad wrapped his arms around her. "I'm sorry, Rachel."

She nodded and pushed him away. "Amy thought you might carve a memorial for me. Do you think you might be able to do a statue of a golden retriever? To put in my garden? Or my living room." She held the tissue to her nose again as tears rolled down her cheeks. "And Garth, if you could do a plaque for my garden."

"Of course," Garth said. "Do you know what you want it to say?"

She pulled a scrap of paper from her pocket and unfolded it before she handed it to him.

"True companion, always in our hearts," Garth read. "I'll start on it right away tomorrow morning."

"I'd be happy to make a statue for you," Thad said. "I've got a piece of granite at the shop that'll be the right size."

Rachel's husband, Hal, approached, head bowed. Thad took a step back and Rachel looked to Hal for comfort.

"We'd be grateful," Hal said. "Send us the bill when you're done."

Garth and Thad both nodded as Hal led Rachel to their booth.

"Sad," Brian said. "You need any help?" he asked Thad. "I could help you get the scrap to your home workshop."

No one went into his home workshop. Not even his brothers. "I think I can manage."

"Speaking of which, Amy stopped by the other night," Garth said as they resumed their seats. "She gave Sandra a catalog of your stuff to put on the website. I was supposed to tell you Sandra should have a new page or two up and running in another day or so."

Thad cringed.

"You did give Amy your approval, didn't you?" Garth asked.

"I did." He took another swallow of beer and squinted at Garth. "Doesn't mean I have to like it."

"Set in your ways," Brian said. "So were dinosaurs."

"Truth," Garth said, raising his mug to toast the statement.

Thad checked Brian's chair—all four legs on the floor—and glowered at him instead. Maybe he *was* finally learning. Instead, Thad reached across and swatted Brian's arm with the back of his hand.

"I still want to see what's in your home workshop," Brian said. "The way you keep everyone out, you'd think there were dead bodies in there or something."

"There's something seriously wrong with you," Thad said, deflecting.

"Think of it as his man cave," Garth said, jumping to Thad's defense. "Guys need a place to hide out once in a while."

"Yeah, but man caves are generally open to other men."

"Give it a rest," Thad said. "It's a workshop, where I don't want to be disturbed or annoyed by outside distractions, including you."

"You ever been inside?" Brian asked Garth.

"I think he just told you it's his private sanctuary," Garth replied. "You've seen the stuff he brings out of there. No dead bodies, only critters and mythical creatures."

"Right," Brian said, leaning on the table. "Like the leprechaun in Amy and Kevin's garden. That's pretty cool. Hey, can you make me a Gollum? You know, the gremlin looking dude from Lord of the Rings."

"If it'll get you to shut up," Thad said. "Where are you going to put it? On Mom and Dad's front lawn?"

Brian scowled and leaned back. "I could move out if you'd pay me more."

"I can't afford to pay you more." Thad wiped a hand across his face. "If this scheme of Amy and Garth's pans out, we could have a run on fountains and garden statues. I'll pay you a stipend to do the installations."

Brian took a swig of his beer and fingered the mug. "You know, I finished my degree."

"You've been going to school for six years," Garth said. "You're never going to finish your degree."

Delia's laugh rang out and Brian pushed away from the table. He charged over to insert himself into whatever conversation she was having with a table full of construction workers.

"Nope, that relationship isn't going to make it to the weekend," Garth said.

Chapter 11

Maggie sat in the cemetery, watching Virginia's headstone from a distance. What hold did the dead girl have over Thad?

The blog was getting more difficult to write. Maggie had promised seven posts, the final one running tomorrow, thank heaven.

Thad Benson, defender of the downtrodden. She'd seen him in the bar last night, but he hadn't seen her. He'd comforted Rachel Morrison, and then a man Maggie supposed was Rachel's husband took over without any male posturing.

In spite of all the gossip around town that had found its way to Maggie about her dinner with Thad, not one person had suggested it might have been romantic. Not. One. Person.

Did the residents of Edgarville see her as one of the downtrodden because of her speech disorder? That would justify Mr. Do-Gooder's interest in her to the general population, but it didn't help her mood.

She'd purposely avoided the café this morning— and missed her cup of blueberry tea.

Hunched over her computer, she agonized over one more installment. The more she found out about Thad Benson, the guiltier she felt about making up a backstory for him and Virginia Carter. So why was she hoping for a glimpse of Thad this morning?

Maggie had crossed the line when she'd kissed him, but it was an innocent kiss. A friendly kiss.

An inviting kiss.

He hadn't accepted her invitation. Probably a good thing considering Maggie didn't know anything about Thad Benson. Not really.

She'd overheard Thad and his brothers talking about his 'man cave,' including the one brother asking him if he kept dead bodies there. She pictured an old episode of Night Gallery with an undertaker who collected indigent dead people to be his family, people the rest of society had forgotten.

Maggie shivered. Thad was not an undertaker. He had a family he was obviously close to. So what was he hiding in his man cave where even his brothers weren't allowed to intrude?

He was turning into an obsession. Or her blog was, the man she'd portrayed him to be—Heathcliff, the tragic hero. One more post and she could leave Thad/Heathcliff behind.

He was a man. A self-proclaimed, confirmed bachelor. No matter how attractive his hero complex was, no matter how interesting his face was, no matter how appealing his physique, he had no romantic interest in Maggie, and he'd made that clear.

Nothing to see here, Mags. Move on.

Which meant she had nothing to lose by looking deeper into the mystery that was Thad Benson.

"Hey, Maggie."

Amy headed toward her, winding her way between the headstones. "Don't usually see people camped out around here. You watching for your mystery man again?"

A quiver of guilt vibrated through Maggie. She didn't dare tell Amy she knew who he was. "Came for the peace and quiet. And inspiration."

Amy raised her face toward the sky, smiled and took a deep breath. "I love being out here. I was raised in the cemetery, what with the family business and all. When the shop is slow, I come out here to enjoy the quiet, too. Wasn't sure I could get away, but my mom stopped in and offered to watch the kids for a few minutes."

"Isn't Thad there?" Maggie asked.

"Thad's working on a project at home," Amy told her.

"How does he work from home? I don't know what all goes into making headstones, but that doesn't seem to be conducive to a home office."

"He does side jobs. Garden statues and stuff like that." She sat beside Maggie on the bench. "Loved your blog post this morning. You know, when I read the first one, I thought the guy was real, but the rest of your posts set me straight. I'm out here a lot, and I don't see any daily visitors. Nobody in town would be pining over a dead girl that way. At least not anyone I know."

Maggie held her breath. What would Amy think when she found out the truth?

Hopefully, no one would ever know.

"Have you ever been to New York?" Amy prattled on. "My husband writes for the newspaper. He has a syndicated column. He's there now, at an AP thing. I figure you must have a similar job, working for the magazine and all."

"No, I've never been to New York," Maggie replied. "My job is social media. I don't write the articles. Different jobs."

Amy rose to her feet. "Am I interrupting you while you're trying to work? I don't know why I'm so chatty today."

Maggie smiled. "I don't mind."

"You want to walk for a bit?" Amy asked.

"Sure." Maggie gathered her things into her tote bag and slung it over her shoulder. "Nice day for it."

Amy crossed the lawn, patting headstones as they went. "You know, the business has been in my family for four generations." She turned to face Maggie. "Thad's the fourth. My other brothers help, but Garth has his own business now, and Brian is working on a degree that will probably take him away from Benson Monuments. Of course, he's been working on a degree for six years." She shrugged. "Not sure he knows what he wants to do."

"What do you do for the business?" Maggie asked.

Amy's expression grew guarded. "My niche is writing epitaphs. I have a knack for it. I like to think I can ease the grief for families who are left behind, give voice to those who have left this realm."

"That's a talent I wish I had," Maggie said. "I never know what to say when people lose a loved one."

"Trust me, it isn't always pleasant." Amy cast a sideways glance at Maggie. "Most people are afraid of ghosts in the cemetery."

Maggie scoffed. "Ghosts. No, I think ghosts are more likely the dear departed that the living are reluctant to let go of. Take my tragic blog hero. I like to think of him as Heathcliff. My guess is he's haunted more by his memories than by an actual ghost."

Amy gave her an odd look, one that said she knew more than she was letting on. She didn't believe in ghosts, did she?

Time to change the subject.

"So your brother, Thad. Does he have a ceramics set-up at home where he makes his garden statues?"

"No, he sculpts them from granite. Or marble. Scrap, usually. He makes headstone ornaments, too, like pets. He's made some beautiful things for the pet cemetery on the other side of town, but… Here. Let me show you." She quickened her pace and headed across one of the roads into another section of the cemetery, stopping beside a grave. On the top of a rectangular headstone, a life-size stone cat lay sleeping.

"The woman who's buried here loved cats." Amy stroked the stone as if it were a real cat. "I can't think of a time when she didn't have them while she was alive. When she passed, I suggested to the family the ornament might be a nice addition and they agreed."

"Thad did this?"

Amy nodded, pride showing on her face. "There are others, but this is one of my favorites."

"And he does this at home? You said scrap stone. That has to be heavy to haul, even such a small piece."

"He doesn't live far—a cottage at the end of Baker Street—and he has a pickup truck." Amy said.

The infamous man cave. "I've heard he doesn't let anyone into his workshop."

"Everyone needs their space, don't you think? For me, it's a walk in the cemetery. For him, it's holing himself up in his workshop." She smiled at Maggie.

"When I heard you two had been to dinner, I was hoping you'd get him out into the world more often. He keeps himself so closed off so much of the time. He's always been sort of a loner, but I'd hate to see him become a hermit. Living out there, at the edge of the woods—it seems such a lonely existence."

Another frisson of apprehension shook through Maggie. "We only had the one dinner. We haven't spoken much since."

"I'm not surprised, but at least you're friends." She nudged Maggie's shoulder.

More than friends? She relived the kiss, inviting him to take the next step. He hadn't bitten. "Sandra said the same thing," Maggie said. "I'm not convinced."

"Hey, I have to get back before my weebies make my mother crazy," Amy said. "Can't wait to read tomorrow's blog."

Maggie had to write that blog post, and she had a book to read. Time to hide away in her rental where she wouldn't be distracted. With one last glance at Virginia Carter's stone, she left the cemetery.

Except instead of driving home, she found herself programming Baker Street into her GPS. Naturally, his house was only a few blocks from the cemetery. Small town.

Baker Street was three blocks long, with a dead end. Maggie parked on the first block and walked the rest of the way so as not to draw attention to her presence. The mid-day humidity wound through her hair, tightening the curls with each step she took.

Amy's description of Thad's house was fairly accurate. At the end of the block, a lone house backed to the woods, an empty lot on either side. Should she knock? Could he see her approach?

What was she doing?

A scraping sound echoed through the trees, following by the tapping of a hammer—a chisel against stone?

Maggie crept toward the woods and spotted the workshop offset from the house, half secluded in Thad's backyard. The door was open, with a dog-sized statue on the walk outside. Maggie ducked behind a tree, held the trunk and leaned around to get a better look.

Thad pulled an apron over his head. He was shirtless, in a pair of shorts. Perspiration created a sheen on his back. Forget Heathcliff. Maggie's thoughts swept to Lady Chatterley's gamekeeper. She stepped away from the tree to get a better look.

Thad set down his tools and took goggles off his head. He picked up a block, smoothing the stone he was working on. He followed the block with his hand, massaging the curve in a move so sensual Maggie's breath caught.

He looked up. Had he heard her?

"Maggie? Is that you?"

Too late to hide behind the trunk again, Maggie took a step forward. "I d-d-d..." Stop. Don't speak. But her brain wasn't cooperating. "I d-i-dn't mean to interrupt." She pointed to the statue of the dog outside the door. "Is this Rachel's Beau?"

He nodded.

Maggie approached and extended a shaking hand to stroke the cool stone surface. "It's beautiful. Very lifelike." She couldn't meet his eyes. "I heard you working and couldn't seem to stop from investigating. I should keep moving, though. I have my own work to do."

"Since you're here." He put one hand on the open door. "You might like to see what I'm working on. It would help explain…" Thad wiped his forehead with the back of his dusty hand.

His body glistened like an oiled body builder wearing not-enough clothes. Maggie struggled to keep her hands off. To make matters worse, his shorts weren't doing an adequate job concealing the part of him currently standing at attention.

Lady Chatterley, indeed. He was inviting her into his lair, which might be filled with dead bodies…

"I know I'm filthy, and probably stinky," he said. "I won't get too close. I promise."

The only odor coming from him was decidedly male musk. "I don't mind," she said quietly. She shook her head struggling to keep up with the conversation. "Explain what?"

He cocked his head to invite her inside once more.

It would be rude to turn him down, wouldn't it? Or foolish.

"The roaming hands the other night," he said.

His current project drew her inside. Maggie came face to face with… "Me?"

Chapter 12

Pride swelled through him. She'd recognized herself in his work. "I hope you're not offended. You have a very expressive face, and…" He couldn't tell her how much he loved the shape of her body. She'd certainly misconstrue his meaning. When she faced him, her eyes glittered. Her gaze dropped south of his waistband. Nothing he could do about that now. He was as hard as the marble he'd been working on.

Maggie ran a finger along the vee at the neckline of her sundress, catching a drop of perspiration before it slid between her breasts.

Thad brushed at the dust on a partially rounded marble shoulder to avoid touching Maggie.

"I'm flattered." The hand she set on his shoulder slid across the sheen on his skin. She stepped into him until her palms rested on his chest.

Time to head this off. "Maggie, I'm not in the market…"

"You're a confirmed bachelor, and you like it that way. I already got the message."

"I'm dirty. And sweaty."

Her gaze locked with his, hot and intent. "I don't care." Her hands traveled down his chest and grazed his shorts with a feather-light touch.

Damn the consequences. He needed relief. "This might sound presumptuous," he said, "but I don't have any protection at hand. It's been a long time since I…"

"Presume away. It's been three years for me, but I'm healthy, and I'm on the pill. It regulates things. So if you want…" She took a step back. "Unless you have something you shouldn't share."

"Nothing that would compromise your health," he said. Thad pressed a kiss to her lips, kicked the workshop door closed, and led her to the workbench. He picked up his gloves, used them to clear a space and lifted her onto the surface. He traced every contour of her arms, memorizing the shape, then cradled her head and leaned forward to kiss her again, tasting her, savoring the warmth of her mouth. She wrapped her legs around him, drawing him closer. At this rate, he was going to lose himself before they started.

Thad eased her skirt up and crouched, settled between her legs and tugged her panties off. He traced the insides of her legs, kissed them, centered himself.

Maggie panted, moaned, bucked, and within moments cried out. Her hands wove into his hair, tugging him to his feet. He eased off his shorts and stepped out of them. As much as he wanted to bury himself inside her, he asked her once more, "You sure you're okay with this?"

She scooted closer, pressing her heat against him. Her hands went to his low back, directing him home.

Eyes closed, he growled and tilted his head while she stretched to take him in. She felt so damn good. Sweat rolled down his back. Thad kissed her once more, stroked her back, nipped at the dots that poked the front of her sundress. As much as he wanted to cup her breasts, he'd leave dusty handprints. He paused, stared into her large eyes, pupils dilated and glazed with lust. He had to see all of her. Thad reached for the hem of her sundress and pulled it over her head.

No bra.

Perfection. He cupped each breast, drew his thumb beneath, across, around. Took each one into his mouth to taste her as his hips drove into her. She moaned and dug her fingers into his shoulders. Her hands glided over his slick skin. She clutched his butt and pulled him deeper. When she cried out once more, tightening around him, he lost all control and gave way to spasms.

He rested his head in the crook of her neck while he caught his breath. "Are you real?" he whispered. "Tell me I didn't imagine this."

She leaned back, met his gaze. Her cheeks were flushed, and her eyes portrayed a less certain expression than he'd seen moments earlier. Regret? Was she going to read more into this than what it was? Expect things from him?

"That was fun," she said. "I'm sorry if I disturbed your work, although I have a hard time apologizing after…" She shot a glance at the likeness of her he was creating. "I hope you'll let me see the statue when it's finished."

Maggie hopped off the workbench and threw her arms into her sundress. Was she leaving?

Did he want her to stay?

"I still owe you a dinner," she said, pulling on her panties. "You'll let me know when you want to collect?"

Part of him wanted to stop her, to invite her inside to shower. To wash off the dirt and sweat. To take this to the bedroom, or for a walk to the tall grass by the creek.

Would she like having sex in the tall grass?

Before he could open his mouth, she kissed him and walked out the door.

Thad slipped on his shorts and started after her. "Maggie."

She stopped. Turned. Arrested his heart. What could he say?

"I'd appreciate it if you don't share what you've seen in my workshop," he said, at a loss for words.

She grinned, twisted two fingers in front of her lips and continued on her way.

Thad dragged a hand through his hair as he watched her disappear up the street, not sure what to make of her, of what they'd done.

But he knew he wanted to do it again.

Chapter 13

Maggie parked in front of her rental and hurried inside. She ran a glass of cold water from the kitchen sink and pressed it to her neck to cool off.

Are you real?

That was the moment Maggie realized her mistake. She'd stepped into a story. Lady Chatterley. Wuthering Heights. Taking advantage of the tragic hero, or the gruff gamekeeper. What had Thad been envisioning?

Virginia Carter.

From her vantage point on the workbench, she'd seen the face looking at her. She recognized her from the yearbook Pru Sawyer had shown her at the café.

What did Maggie know about Thad Benson? For all she knew, he kept a blow-up doll in his workshop and gave it a poke while he was staring into the face of Virginia Carter. And who were the other women's faces staring at her?

Are you real?

If she was honest, she'd been with the proverbial someone else, too.

He had a full-body clay miniature of her. Her face was recognizable in the stone counterpart. She could still feel his hands on her, running across her skin, squeezing as if testing for size and texture. Knowing

90

every sensitive spot, lingering. He'd worshipped her body as if she was the Venus de Milo. With arms.

She'd fantasized about Thad Benson, but she'd never expected to realize those fantasies. She was a forty-one-year-old woman.

They were in Edgarville, where everyone knew everyone else's business. For all she knew, someone had seen them, spied on them, the same way she'd been spying on Thad. Their tryst could be all over town by tomorrow. Worse, he'd kicked her libido into high gear.

Thank you, sir, may I have another?

She giggled. *Could* she ask Thad for a repeat performance? Did that make her a sexual predator? What if he turned out to be a stalker? There had to be a reason he was a confirmed bachelor.

Thad Benson was a do-gooder. If he was a predator, he wouldn't have asked if she was 'sure.' He would have plundered her without any thought to her needs, and he'd definitely taken her needs into consideration. What would have happened if she *hadn't* envisioned him as Heathcliff, or as the gamekeeper?

Damn it all, she wanted another chance—a do-over.

Technically, it was like buying dinner. He'd bought dinner that first night, but he hadn't argued when she'd offered to return the favor. If logic followed, he'd bought her a different kind of a dinner this time. Should she offer reciprocation?

If he took her up on her offer to pay for their next dinner, and that was a big if, she could float the friends with benefits idea. Tell him how much she'd enjoyed their interlude and suggest they go another round. Somewhere out of town to avoid the rumor mill—

assuming anyone gave her credit for seducing the town's confirmed bachelor.

On the other hand, did she want to be his blow-up doll?

Maybe moving to Edgarville was a mistake. Her rental was month-to-month, until she found a more permanent place, but she could go back to Foxfield. Commute.

No. Torie needed her own space to have her own life, and so did Maggie. If they continued to live together, they'd grow into spinsters, use each other as an excuse not to date. They both deserved a chance at a family and a happily ever after.

Maggie liked everyone she'd met in Edgarville so far, including Thad Benson. Sandra. Amy. Rachel. Okay, Pru was no prize, but they were nice, ordinary people. Neighbors were allowed to be nosy when they were looking out for one another.

What would they say when they found out Thad was the star of her blog posts?

Would they find out? If they didn't recognize him from what she'd written, chances were he'd kept his secret obsession well hidden.

Or Maggie had invented something from nothing.

Had he and Virginia only been friends?

She had more questions than answers, and still more questions waiting to be asked. All those questions could be answered—if she asked the appropriate people. Starting with Thad.

Guilt flushed through her once more. She'd taken a man's moment of solitude and put it on the world stage.

She could fix this. She had one more post to write, and she could script her own ending, the same way she'd scripted her tragic hero.

Maggie crossed to the kitchen table and turned her computer on. She typed a scenario where Thad bent over the stone, laid flowers at the grave, and was greeted by another woman. A wife. The dead girl's sister. Or daughter.

Did the dead girl have a sister? And at nineteen, she wasn't likely to have had a daughter, but it was certainly possible. Not one person had suggested Virginia had a moral compass. Pregnancy was certainly a possibility. Maggie could make Thad a father in her imaginary world.

Muscles taut, Maggie deleted the wife and/or daughter, overcome by an unexpected wave of jealousy.

Because he'd slept with her? She'd hardly known the man a week.

Maggie pushed away from the table, staring at her computer screen.

There would be no reciprocal dinner. There would be no friends with benefits. Maggie predicted more days in the office and less working from home or, as had become her new routine, less days working in the café or in the cemetery.

She glanced at the books on the end table beside the sofa. One of the novels might inspire Maggie to write a happy ending for Thad Benson, one that didn't include his large hands, or the cords of muscle glistening on a hot summer's evening, or his head between her legs.

Maggie shot to her feet and walked to the window, cupping her chin while she blew out a slow breath, hoping to blow away her visit to Thad's workshop as easily.

It was a fluke. She'd been three years without a man-induced orgasm and Mr. First Available, Mr. Do-Gooder, had merely reminded her how good it felt. Nothing more. Who cared if he was haunted by his memories of a dead woman?

He'd started sculpting a statue of Maggie, and while she'd watched him smooth the curves of stone, she'd projected the feeling of his hands on her. Seemed like a rational explanation. Sex was as much mental as it was physical. Her imagination had been in high gear, and clearly, his had been, too, after working on his art.

He'd been sculpting a statue of her.

Her phone rang and she nearly jumped out of her skin. Maggie snatched it off the table, grateful for the distraction from her runaway thoughts. "Hello?"

"I'm guessing you want an explanation." Thad's gravelly voice raised gooseflesh.

How did he do that to her? She was halfway to orgasm just listening to him talk. *Play it cool*. "For?" she asked.

"What you saw. What I did. What we did."

She closed her eyes, letting his voice seep into her. "I didn't think confirmed bachelors were in the habit of explaining themselves," she teased, her cheeks hot. "Two consenting adults?" One of whom wanted to consent more. Damn her libido.

"Now that I've had a chance to shower, I thought we could talk," he said.

"Men don't normally like talking, and while I haven't known you long, I do know you're a man of few words to begin with." Not to mention she couldn't sit in the same room with him in this condition without peeling off more clothes—his and hers—and he was calling to "explain." Code word for backtrack. Or apologize.

She didn't want apologies. No regrets.

"I have work to do," she said. "For the magazine. But I did offer to buy you dinner, to return the favor. Tomorrow night?" The last blog post would be completed by then, and if she removed her imagination from the equation, he'd stop appearing to her as Heathcliff.

"You caught me by surprise," he said.

That made two of them.

"And left me tongue tied," he went on.

"As I remember, your tongue worked just fine," she said, eyes closed. Maggie smacked her forehead. Verbal foreplay was not the answer right now.

Thad chuckled. "I have to admit, I'd hoped you'd join me in the shower. Clean up and try again like civilized people."

"Are you, sir, calling me uncivilized?" she joked.

"I'm saying you appeal to my baser instincts," he replied. "As much as I enjoyed our interlude, I have to consider it might not have been what you were looking for. Which begs the question, why did you stop by my house this afternoon?"

To get a glimpse of him in his man cave. To satisfy her Lady Chatterley curiosity. He'd come through in spades. He was still flirting with her, leaving the door open for more chapters in their erotic story. Maggie shot a glance at the books she still needed to read, books she could read tomorrow.

Laughter outside the window reminded her where she was. Edgarville. "I could tell you I lost my way this afternoon," she said, "but that would be a lie. A little bird told me about your workshop and I was curious." She licked her lips and took a deep breath. "Which leads me to point out the obvious, that this is a small town where everybody knows everybody else. If I invite you over, if I come to your house, as much as people scoffed at the idea of us having a romantic dinner together, they'd likely reconsider if they saw my car parked outside your house all night."

"I think you've already experienced what people will say. Unless they paint us as Beauty and the Beast?" he said with a laugh.

"Which one is the beast?" she asked.

"Did I neglect to tell you how lovely you are? I hope you don't mind the sculpture."

What was she supposed to say? She was still stunned.

"You're worried about what people will say," he repeated.

"It's your community," she pointed out. "They hardly know me. You're the one who will suffer from the gossip."

"The part about where I'm keeping the company of a pretty woman? I think I can live with that. What's this really about, Maggie? Regrets?"

"Not a one." No, she wouldn't change one minute of the afternoon. Except the part about wondering if he was replacing her for Virginia Carter—looking for a new blow-up doll.

"Your reputation?"

Maggie flapped her lips. "Can I point out the fact that after seeing you and me at dinner together, no one I've met thinks there's a chance of anything romantic happening between us? What reputation?"

"That's the confirmed bachelor thing." He sighed. "You did say you had fun. I only called because I did, too, and I thought we might…"

"Have more fun?" she supplied, her voice failing her.

He didn't answer.

To hell with second-guessing herself. She was a single woman, entitled to take what joy she could find in her life. She needed a second chance to ground her in the real world instead of the fantasy she'd created. "Hey, if the gossips don't bother you, I can come back, but I can't stay long. I do have work to do."

"I'll be waiting."

He disconnected.

He wasn't kidding.

She didn't care. She wanted to see him as Thad Benson and not as a hero who'd stepped out of a novel.

Maggie grabbed her purse and keys and headed out, driving to Baker Street. Screw what the neighbors thought. She didn't want to walk home after dark, even in a friendly town like Edgarville.

She arrived at Thad's house inside of five minutes, gave herself one more pep talk, and walked to the front door. There was no question what she wanted, and he'd offered himself to her on a platter. They'd get naked, do the horizontal mambo one more time and the novelty would wear off. No gamekeeper dripping with sweat. No statues looking on. No stone carvings, just a man and a woman and two bodies, satisfying a primal urge.

Take out the imagination part and it would be purely mechanical. Right?

Thad opened the door, a bottle of beer in his hand, wearing a clean pair of running shorts and nothing else. "Wasn't sure you'd come."

What did she know about him? He might still be a stalker, or a hundred other variations of a 'bad guy.'

No, whatever else Thad Benson was, he was a do-gooder. "Would have been rude to turn down such a tempting invitation."

He stepped aside and she walked in. Built-in bookshelves lined one wall of his living room. A well-worn gray sofa with end tables was set at a right angle to divide the room from the open kitchen. Two of the dinette chairs occupied corners in the living room and a flat screen television was mounted to the wall over a fireplace.

Maggie walked to the bookshelves and ran a hand over the titles. He'd built four bookshelves—or she assumed he'd built them—and in each there was a section dedicated to curios, figures carved from stone. The rest of the shelves were lined with books. Mystery authors. Legal thrillers. Moby Dick. Grapes of Wrath. Wuthering Heights.

He's not Heathcliff.

"I wasn't trying to be crass," he said, setting the beer on an end table. "And if you came here to set me straight, I'd understand."

Mr. Do-Gooder confirmed. He wasn't backing her into a corner. He was still giving her the opportunity to walk away. A man who read. A man with an overabundance of testosterone that sent its tentacles out to draw her in.

Maggie pulled her sundress over her head and stood before him wearing nothing but skin. "I think you said something about acting like civilized people, but you know what? I don't particularly care how we do it." She reached a hand to his pecs, leaned in to inhale the scent of his soap.

"You sure you're okay with this?" he asked, his skin rippling beneath her touch.

She took a step back and held out her hands. "Do I look like I'm not okay with this?" She nodded at his shorts. "You, on the other hand, are overdressed."

While he stepped out of his shorts, he leaned in to kiss her, pulling her close when his hands were free. "Sometimes civilized just means clean," he said.

Hours later, Maggie opened her eyes and rolled over to look at the clock. Four a.m.?

Beside her, Thad made noises like a motorboat in the no-wake area. She hadn't intended to stay. The longer she did, the worse it would be for her. Everyone in town would know if she spent the night, and it was only a matter of time before they discovered that not only was Thad the man in the cemetery, she'd taken advantage of him. The people of Edgarville were going to look at *her* as the predator.

She slid out of bed and tiptoed to the living room to retrieve her sundress. Time to go home. Maggie stubbed her toe on a video cabinet. As she bent to massage her injured foot, she glanced at the titles. *Beauty and the Beast. Brave. Hook.* Disney movies? On the shelf below, she found the shoot-'em-up action movies she might expect from a man. She looked over her shoulder, at the bedroom she'd left.

Thad Benson was a contradiction, a puzzle, one she didn't dare try to figure out. She'd taken advantage of him, and sooner or later she was going to have to pay the price.

Chapter 14

Thad wasn't surprised when he'd woken alone. After the hours he'd shared with Maggie, he'd half-hoped she would stay the night.

In her shoes, he wouldn't want to wake up to his face, either.

She *had* said she couldn't stay long.

She'd stayed longer than he'd expected. Now they'd have to deal with the awkward meeting on the street the next time they saw each other which, he hoped, would be today.

It was time he learned more about Maggie Grant.

With a cup of coffee and a bowl of cereal at his kitchen table, Thad opened his computer and found the magazine web page. Amy had mentioned Maggie wrote a blog, that she had a romantic soul.

The blog was easy enough to find. He read while he ate. Maggie was definitely a romantic. The subject of her blog, apparently a series she'd written through the week, was a character study of Heathcliff in Wuthering Heights applied to a man she'd seen pining after a lost lover. She expressed how tender the man's emotions felt, even from a distance, how every day he laid a bouquet of wildflowers before the dead girl's stone.

To imagine a love so strong as to endure the separation of death, the devotion of someone twenty years later, is to know that good men do exist in this world. They deserve someone better than Catherine to love. This man makes me want to be a better woman, a more loving partner.

Pretty words, but a more loving partner wouldn't disappear in the middle of the night.

What could he expect? Maggie was gorgeous, at least in his eyes. And he was... well, Amy called him a troglodyte. Did Maggie have another 'loving partner?'

Time to stop dwelling on what he'd shared with Maggie. Thad set his spoon in the bowl and browsed the headlines of the previous six posts. They'd have to wait. He had a statue to deliver.

He rinsed his dishes and set them in the sink before he walked out to the workshop, loaded "Beau" into his pickup and headed to the monument shop.

Amy was there when he arrived, with both kids and his mother.

"Do you people realize today is Sunday?" he said. "And aren't you supposed to be retired?" he asked his mom.

"I am. I'm enjoying my grandchildren."

"You should all be at the park." He leaned over Amy and took the headstone order folder from her desk.

She grabbed it from him. "I forgot my phone yesterday, which explains why I'm here. This order will keep until tomorrow. And you're here because?"

"Need to deliver Beau to Rachel. Had to pass the shop anyway." The folder only held one headstone order but he felt compelled to complete it, to do something to keep the monument shop solvent. He should be happy his friends and neighbors weren't dropping dead, but one stone wasn't going to pay the bills.

"Who wants to go to the park?" his mother asked.

Both kids responded like dogs being asked if they wanted to go for a walk.

"I'll meet you there," Amy said. She held the door as they walked out, and then turned to Thad.

Thad glanced at Amy's computer. She'd been reading Maggie's blog. "Doesn't look like work," he said.

"She has such a way with words. I can't help but wonder who the man is she's writing about," she said.

Thad smirked. "A figment of her imagination, no doubt. You should know better than anyone who comes and goes at Mount Hope."

Amy scowled and closed her browser. "I don't see everything that goes on over there. You have no soul, Thad Benson, but then what would I expect from my troglodyte brother?"

He winced. The barb hurt more than usual today. He snatched the stencil Amy had printed from the folder and carried it into the workshop.

"You okay?" she asked a moment later, standing at his shoulder.

"Yeah. Why?"

"You seem different."

"Same troll I am every day," he said without looking at her.

"It's pronounced troglodyte, like caveman."

"Yeah, well, you've got Kevin to stand over you with a club these days."

"Which he doesn't do," she said. "Because he knows I don't need to be protected from every person I come into contact with. A lesson my brothers never learned."

He cocked his eyebrows. "There were times you were grateful we were there."

She slid her arms around his waist and hugged him. "I'm grateful for you every day."

The shot of nostalgia hit him hard. In spite of her brothers, Amy had found her own way. Now she had kids of her own, and so did Garth. The family had grown, and things had changed. He missed hanging out with his brothers, standing watch over Amy.

"Listen," she said as she pulled away. "Kevin's coming home this afternoon and I was wondering if you can babysit for an hour or two. We have a few things to catch up on. Mom and Dad have some 'thing' they have to go to, and Garth and Sandra are taking Zach to the zoo."

An hour or two. Thad nodded. "Yeah. I'm working on a project, but it can wait until later."

She hugged him once more before she traipsed to the showroom.

Thad found the headstone that went with the order and applied the stencil. He pulled on his gloves to hoist the stone onto a dolly, wishing one of his brothers was hanging around.

Babysitting. The best part about kids—and family—was they were accustomed to their family's appearance. Chloe and Randall loved him, even if the nicest thing anyone said about his face—even his own mother—was 'it had character.'

Thad yanked his gloves off and slammed them against the stone.

He stormed through the shop. "Going for a cup of coffee," he called over his shoulder.

He was forty-two years old. He'd lived with this face all his life. Why was it bothering him now?

By the time he'd reached the coffee shop, he knew the answer.

She was there. Maggie. And darn if his heart didn't jerk. Thad shook his head. It wasn't his heart that was involved, his problem was further south.

He wasn't an adolescent. So why did he feel like one?

He walked inside and strolled calmly to the counter.

"Morning, Thad," Sandra said. "Coffee? I need to make a fresh pot if you don't mind waiting a minute or two. I have to grab a box from the back."

"That's fine."

While Sandra disappeared into the kitchen, he turned and found Maggie watching him, a book in her hand.

"Morning," he said.

"Thad."

"Didn't get a chance to say thanks," he said.

Maggie raised her eyebrows. "Not required. Otherwise I'd have to thank you, too." She smiled. "Thank you."

Amy walked into the café and stopped halfway to the counter. She glanced between Thad and Maggie, a question in her eyes. The rumor mill was probably churning. Even though his neighbors weren't right next door, they would have noticed the car in the driveway.

She managed a friendly smile. "Hi, Maggie. I heard you paid my big brother a call yesterday."

Maggie speared Thad with a glance. Did she think he'd said something?

"She's sitting for me," he said.

"Sitting for you?" Amy echoed.

"You are the one who said I should do more garden statues."

Amy's face screwed up. "I'm not following."

"Thought I'd try my hand at something bigger. A real statue. Maggie agreed to sit for me."

Amy's eyebrows winged upward. She glanced at Sandra, who had returned from the kitchen with a box of coffee and laughed.

"Well, that explains it," Amy said. "For a minute, I actually thought you might be human."

Not what he needed to hear today.

Maggie held his gaze with an inscrutable look on her face. Understanding? Thanks? Pity?

"I was intrigued when you told me about his man-cave workshop," Maggie told Amy. "Have to admit I was curious. He was kind enough to show me around." Her expression was tight. Tense. Was she angry? At him?

"A real statue, huh?" Sandra said. "I published a new web page with the pictures Amy took. You'll have to let me know when you finish so I can add that, too. Who knows? We might discover we have a Donatello on our hands."

Amy broke into the Teenage Mutant Ninja Turtles theme song. So now he was a mutant.

How long did coffee take to brew? Sandra seemed to be moving at turtle pace ripping open a bag from the box of coffee and pouring it into the filter. Thad folded his arms and studied the pastries.

He wasn't hungry.

Amy continued to Maggie's table. "Your blog was so sweet today. We should all want to be better women. Better people."

Starting with family, Thad wanted to add, but she couldn't know how her words affected him today. It was everyday banter, things he'd heard a thousand times before. No need to overreact.

Except when Maggie had stopped over yesterday, he *had* felt human, for the first time in more years than he cared to remember. And he'd liked it. Today, not so much. Did Maggie feel sorry for him? Was she taking advantage of him? Hell, he'd started it. He couldn't blame her. If he was honest with himself, he'd used her, too, like Ginny and he had used each other all those years ago. Ginny had never tried to sugarcoat it. For that matter, Maggie hadn't either.

He wasn't quite sure what to think about Maggie.

Thad had given up on sex years ago. He'd run the gamut, from women who were curious about his size—he was taller than the average man, after all—to women who didn't know how to say no and cried later, to Maggie. Where did she fit in the grand scheme of things?

He might have taken advantage of her when he'd found her snooping around his workshop, but she'd come back. Not a crier. And she'd stayed. Not all night, but for more than "one quick one and I have to go." She'd been wildly passionate, not closing her eyes against an ugly face—although it *had* been dark.

They'd gone a couple of rounds before they'd exhausted themselves.

He would have gone at least once more had she stayed to sunup.

"Here you go, Thad," Sandra said, saving him from his thoughts.

He took the cup and nodded, handing over a couple of bucks.

"Did you want me to sit for you today?" Maggie asked before he reached the door.

Thad shot a look at Amy. "I'm babysitting for Amy, but you did mention dinner. If you want to stop by then, I'll throw in a pizza. Otherwise, we can figure out another day."

Maggie's lips curled into a smile and her features relaxed. "It's up to you."

"Might as well strike while the muse is hot," he said.

The flash in her eyes indicated she was, indeed, hot. "As long as you don't mind me reading while you work," she added innocently.

Nice touch. "Makes for a good statue," he said. "A woman reading."

"Then I'll see you later."

Maggie made him feel like a Hollywood movie star.

Better not read too much into it. She'd get tired of his face soon enough.

Chapter 15

Maggie gathered her things, smiled politely at Amy, Sandra and Thad, and left the café. Time to hide away in her rental and lose herself in a book or two.

Instead of birds fluttering inside, she prickled with irritation.

She analyzed what Amy had said, what Sandra had said, what Thad had said. Way more than was absolutely necessary.

Point number one. Thad had said he didn't care about the gossips, and yet, when Amy started probing, Thad invented a plausible explanation for the way Maggie had stalked him.

Yes, she was the stalker.

She covered her face with her hand and shook her head.

Which one of them was he trying to protect? She'd been the one to point out the small town angle, how tongues would wag. Thad had told Maggie people wouldn't expect that from him and he'd been right. Where else in the world would people disregard such an obvious late night booty call?

Point number two. While Amy had seemed suspicious at first, Thad's explanation was taken without question. Because Maggie wasn't pretty enough? Because Maggie had a speech disorder which, even if she conquered it most of the time, was still evident? Even to the casual observer? Or—and this point annoyed her even more than being personally insulted—had Amy's comment about Thad being human been as offensive to him as it had been to her? She'd seen Thad cringe in response. Yes, families often took playful jabs at each other, but to Maggie's way of thinking—and judging from Thad's response—Amy had crossed a line.

Amy had said Thad didn't have a romantic bone in his body. She was wrong, of course, but was she so blind? She hadn't even questioned the idea of Maggie modeling for him. Plenty of statues were unclothed. What would Amy say if Maggie showed up to Thad's house naked?

No. Bad idea. There would be children present.

The Disney movies in Thad's collection made more sense. If he regularly babysat for Amy's kids, he'd likely seen Beauty and the Beast multiple times. An easy joke.

He didn't consider himself a beast, did he? In her experience, men didn't think about their appearance the way women did.

When she reached her rental, her phone rang. Torie.

"Hey, what are you doing next weekend?" Torie asked while Maggie unlocked the door. "I've been offered tickets to the Scott Michaels concert in Chicago Friday night and thought you might like to go along. What do you say?"

Maggie dropped her things inside and leaned on the kitchen counter. "I didn't know he was touring again after DragonPurr broke up."

"C'mon, you know you want to," her sister said. "You've got to be bored to tears over there in Smalltown America. I read your blog. A more loving partner. When's the last time you had sex, Maggie?"

"Last night."

Torie gasped. "You've got my attention."

Maggie chuckled.

"Come on. Details."

Maggie lowered her voice. "Six foot huge and oozing testosterone. Mr. Do-Gooder. Strong, silent, a voice like George Clooney. Champion of the downtrodden with a heart of gold. Confirmed bachelor."

"Even George found himself a bride." Torie said. "Are we talking about the Heathcliff guy who inspired your blog?"

"Up close and personal," Maggie said quietly.

Torie laughed. "I guess you won't want that ticket, then. You've got better things to do than drool over a rock star with me."

"Well, here's the downside," Maggie said. "This is Smalltown America."

"Where everybody knows everybody's business," Torie finished.

"Funny thing is they seem to think he's asexual. Over the hill or just plain not interested. The people here have been very welcoming, but once they find out he's the guy in my blog, I might be ostracized. I'm seriously considering moving back to Foxfield where I can blend into the woodwork, where I won't disappoint anyone when they find out I've put this guy's private grief on display for the world to read."

"You mean they don't recognize him from your posts?" Torie asked.

"They don't give him any credit for being a living, breathing, human being. I guarantee you, he is nowhere near as out of order as they perceive him to be."

"Out of order. I like that." Torie sighed. "Maybe I'll take a pass on those tickets, too and come visit you, instead. Unless your not-out-of-order Heathcliff has other plans for you. Bwa-ha-ha." She gasped again. "Wait a minute. Back up to the part where he's a confirmed bachelor, and the part in your blog where he's pining over a dead woman."

Maggie frowned. "Men have urges, even if he can't get said dead woman out of his mind. He asked me if I was real. What does that say to you?"

"That the sex was mind blowing. That it was so good, he wasn't sure if it was a fantasy."

"Or he was haunted by the dead woman and wasn't actually 'with' me. She might be the reason he's a confirmed bachelor. Other women are placeholders that he slaps the dead girl's face on."

"Is that what you think?" Torie asked.

Maggie grabbed a handful of hair. "I don't know. I wish I could be sure."

"So, Friday night? A concert might take your mind off things. Or I could come there and you could show me around Smalltown. Introduce me to Mr. Do-Gooder with the George Clooney voice."

"You go to the concert," Maggie said. "I know how much you love Scott Michaels. Take that man of yours, but we should plan to get together."

"Wouldn't be the same without you. I'll call you later in the week to twist your arm some more. And I want to hear more about this guy."

"Fair enough. Talk to you then."

Maggie carried her book to the nondescript sofa. The furnished rental was comfortable enough, but she missed her own things. She had yet to stop into the real estate office. Was she procrastinating?

Did she want to move to Edgarville?

The easy answer was yes, but she couldn't deny she was afraid of the repercussions if people discovered Thad was the subject of her blog.

Today was the final installment. In another week, people would forget all about her stupid blog.

For now, she had work to do. Maggie curled into the corner of the sofa and opened the book.

The next time the phone rang, she was three-quarters the way through the story.

"Uh-huh?" she answered, trying to get to the end of the paragraph before the conversation took over.

"Hey," Jean said. "I'm on my way to Foxfield, but I'm going right by Edgarville. Did a 10K this morning and I'm starving. Want to get lunch? Or have you already eaten?"

Maggie marked her place with a bookmark and set the book down. "What time is it?"

Jean laughed. "I'm guessing you're reading."

"I am, which means I haven't eaten yet, so yes. Stop by and we'll go out for something." Would she run into Thad at the café again? "You know what, I haven't tried the pub yet. I hear it's good. What do you think?"

"Sounds perfect. I'll meet you there in fifteen minutes?"

"Yep," Maggie said, reaching for her notebook. She set her phone down and scribbled review notes, along with a couple of passages she'd marked to quote. With the book tucked into her purse, she started for the pub.

When she reached Murphy's, Jean was pulling into a parking space on the street in front. Maggie waited for Jean to get out and gave her a hug before they walked inside.

The pub was full of people, most of them gathered around the bar watching the Cubs game. A woman in a waitress uniform and a nametag that read "Delia" greeted them. "Take a seat wherever you can find one," she said. "Menus are on the table. I'll be by to get your order in a few minutes."

"Thank you," Jean said.

As they turned sideways through the crowd at the bar, Maggie bumped a large man, almost as large as Thad. "Excuse me," she said.

"No problem," he grumbled, a frown on his face. A face that looked too much like Thad's. The third brother.

"Somethin' wrong?" he asked when she'd stared too long.

"You look so much like…" She swallowed. "You must be one of the Bensons."

His frown disappeared into a smile. "Brian." He held out his hands. "And you are?"

"Maggie." She turned. "And my friend, Jean."

Jean wiggled beside her and took Brian's extended hand, looking into his face with something akin to awe.

114

"Nice to meet you, Brian," she said, her voice taking on a different tone than Maggie was used to hearing. Was she flirting?

Brian responded, closing his other hand over hers. "Jean, was it? A pleasure." He shifted a quick glance to Maggie, but seemed to have trouble tearing himself away from Jean's intent gaze. "You're the one who had dinner with Thad?" he asked.

"Guilty," Maggie said.

"Would you like to join us for lunch?" Jean asked, then looked to Maggie. "If you don't mind."

Maggie shrugged. "No problem here." She had a hunch Jean wouldn't be going home to Foxfield tonight.

He accompanied them to a booth and took a seat beside Jean. Maggie reached for the menus and passed them around.

Brian kept his focus on Jean. He'd figured out which one of them was interested.

"What do you recommend?" Jean asked.

"It's all good," he said.

Delia appeared by the table and gave them a guarded look. "Can I get you something to drink?" she asked.

Brian took Jean's hands in his. "Let me buy," he said.

"Coke," Jean said, not looking at Delia.

"Water for me," Maggie said.

"You know what I want," Brian said, sending a significant look to Delia. She nodded and walked away.

What had Sandra told her about Brian and the barmaid? Maggie should tell Jean what she'd heard before things went much further.

"Have you lived here long?" Jean asked.

"All my life, but I'm thinking it's time to move on," Brian said.

"Where would you go?"

Brian glanced at Maggie. "Just finished my degree. What with working and going to school, it took longer than expected, but now that I have it, I plan to find myself a job somewhere else." He checked the spot Delia had vacated. "My girlfriend moved on to someone new, my big brother took over the family business. Nothing here for me anymore. I'll be more successful someplace else."

So much for his relationship with the barmaid.

He looked at Jean once more and smiled. "Where you from?"

"I live in Foxfield. The magazine I work for moved here, and I've been commuting."

"Foxfield sounds like a friendly place," Brian said. "I should check it out."

Delia arrived with their drinks, in time to prevent Maggie from sticking her finger down her throat and gagging.

Maybe she should skip lunch and let the two of them fawn over each other—in front of the girlfriend who'd moved on, if Delia was, in fact, that girlfriend. This couldn't end well.

"The trouble I'm having," Brian said, "is that I don't know how to tell my brothers. See, we all work together in the family business, and I feel sort of like I'd be leaving them high and dry." He took a sip of his beer. "On the other hand, business isn't so good these days. I'd probably be doing them a favor by leaving."

Jean shimmied in the small space beside him and reached for her coke. "What do you do?"

"My family owns a monument business. Four generations. I figure my brothers have it under control."

He smiled at Jean and clinked his mug to her glass. "Here's to new beginnings."

No one offered to toast Maggie's water glass. She was definitely a third wheel, familiar territory. "You know what?" she said. "I have an appointment and I didn't realize how late it was getting. Jean, I hate to bail on you, but do you mind if I skip lunch?"

Jean didn't even have the good grace to look away from Brian. "No, you go on ahead. Brian can keep me company."

Maggie quirked an eyebrow.

"If you don't mind," Jean added, batting her eyelashes at Brian.

"Don't mind at all," he said, leaning closer to her.

Yep. Definitely going to gag. Thank heaven she hadn't ordered a real drink, or food. "Nice to meet you, Brian. I'll talk to you tomorrow, Jean."

Jean wagged her eyebrows at Maggie. They'd have lots to talk about by then.

So Thad's brother was bailing on him. Why couldn't Maggie get away from the Bensons? If she was smart, she'd skip going to Thad's tonight. With the town watching, someone would figure out modeling wasn't the only thing she was doing with him.

What, exactly, was she doing with him? Thad was in love with a ghost.

No, she'd go to her rental and finish reading the damn book she was scheduled to review. Except when she stopped walking, she found herself at the corner of Baker Street.

That man had way too much testosterone.

Might as well enjoy what they had while they had it. She'd move back to Foxfield, where it wouldn't be so convenient to stop over.

The problem lay in the fact she was beginning to care about Thad Benson. About the way he'd reacted to his sister's barbs. The way his brother was going to walk out on him and the family business.

As she approached his cottage, she heard voices, Thad's and a little girl singing about little speckled frogs. She peered through the window. Thad sat on the floor, a small boy perched on his shoulders. The scene was so sweet she hesitated to knock.

How could such a caring man be in love with a woman like Virginia Carter? Everyone in town had something unkind to say about the dead girl, including the men. Thad must have chosen to remember only the good things, as people will of the dead, but he had to know what kind of girl Virginia was.

Maggie turned to leave. She had no business toying with Thad Benson, the confirmed bachelor.

Amy came toward her, accompanied by a spark plug of a man with hair the color of a copper penny and striking sea green eyes.

"Hey, Maggie," Amy said. "This is my husband, Kevin."

Maggie shook Kevin's hand. "Nice to meet you."

"Same," he said.

"I hope I'm not late," Amy said. "You think Thad will let me see the sculpture?"

Thad opened the door, the little boy giggling on his shoulders. "You're early," he said to Maggie.

"I c-c-could come back later." The tell-tale stutter.

"No sense in that," Amy said. "We're here now."

"And no," Thad told Amy. "You can't see the sculpture. Not until it's done."

Maggie's skin rippled with the tenor of his voice.

She was way more involved with the confirmed bachelor than she ought to be.

Chapter 16

T had lifted Chloe over his head to squeals of delight and brought her down for a hug before he set her on the ground. Amy hoisted Randall to her hip. He reached a tiny fist toward Thad and Thad offered a finger. Randall latched onto it with a big smile and a giggle. The gesture wrapped around Thad's heart as easily as Randall's tiny fist wrapped around Thad's finger.

"Take care of your mother, my man," he said, leaning in to kiss the top of Randall's head.

"Thanks for watching them," Amy said. "I'll get out of your way." She looked over her shoulder as she headed for the door. "I'm dying to see the statue. I'm going to want to take a photo for your portfolio, you know."

"You've got first dibs," he said. He held the door for her and watched her all the way to the car. After she'd gotten the kids buckled in, she waved once more before Kevin drove them off.

Thad closed the door and turned to Maggie. She held one of Randall's toys in her hand, studying it, a frown on her face.

"Everything okay?" he asked.

She looked up and set the toy to one side. "Trying to decide if I should be insulted."

Huh? "Why would you be insulted?"

"I have a hard time wrapping my head around your sister completely discounting the possibility that this is more than you've suggested."

"This?"

"My being here. Alone with you. Sandra, too. Neither of them even hinted we might be…" she pursed her lips and exhaled loudly through her nose. "Doing what we're doing."

Thad laughed. "Are you complaining? I thought you didn't want to be the subject of gossip."

"I don't, but for them to completely discount the idea…"

"That we're having sex?" he supplied for her.

She nodded.

Maggie had a point, a sharp point if the stab in his chest was any indication. "I haven't dated in years, and they don't have any reason to doubt what I told them. Why should that be insulting to you?"

"They either consider you not human or I'm not a woman someone like you would be interested in."

She didn't believe that, did she? "I think you've got that backward."

"I saw the look on your face at the café when she called you a troglodyte."

Thad cringed. His face. The one that had character. "Maybe we should go out to the workshop. Now that I've given you an excuse to be here, I should take advantage of the opportunity to have you actually sit for me."

"Wouldn't want anyone to get the wrong idea." Her voice was laced with sarcasm.

What was he missing? Was she going to ask for a commitment? Demand things from him?

Maggie shook her head as if dismissing the subject. "You'd mentioned a statue of a woman reading." She held her prop in the air. "I brought a book."

Did she want to be associated with him romantically?

Even if that was true, she was bound to come to her senses and realize she was out of his league.

He cast a glance at his bedroom door, more than a little disappointed, but he wouldn't make her do anything as distasteful as pretending his looks didn't matter. "All right."

He walked through the kitchen and opened the back door, extending a hand for her to pass. Maggie hesitated, watching him too closely.

"I know some families have certain dynamics," she said. "Things you say and ways you act that are normal. Me, too. I have a sister I don't get along all that well with. I have a friend who fights with her sister all the time, and that's normal for them. It's how they get along. I'm sorry if I read something more into Amy's comments."

No, she'd read it right. Amy had no reason to think Thad might have a life outside the monument shop, that he might have impulses and urges like any other man. He wiped his mouth with his hand. "I'm sure she never considered you might misconstrue what she said." He also wasn't the kind of man women gravitated toward.

Maggie walked toward the open door and stopped beside him rather than pass through. "Then she was insulting you?"

Her words stabbed his chest once more. "I don't suppose my sister thinks about me in those terms."

"Having sex?" Maggie's silky voice slid over him once more, lighting his nerve endings.

"Yes."

"At the risk of ruining a perfectly good thing, I probably wouldn't expect it, either," she said in a softer voice. "Considering we've known each other, what? A week?"

Here it comes. Was she telling him she didn't want any more bedroom interludes?

Maggie stepped inside his personal space and laid a hand on his chest. His body responded, traitor that it was. She looked him in the eye. "I don't know what it is, Thad, but when we're together, it's not just sex."

She *wasn't* telling him she was done? He was having a hard time keeping up.

"I know you're a confirmed bachelor. I'm not pressing you for more than you're willing to give me, but I have to be honest with you." She searched his eyes and he felt it deep in his soul. "I hardly know you. You hardly know me, but there's more to this than sex."

He swallowed hard, more confused than ever.

"I'll sit for you, if that's all you want," she went on. "But gossip or no, you should know I hope whatever else it is we're doing continues, as well."

She was still looking into his face. *Seeing* his face. "That sounds like an invitation," he said, his voice cracking.

She smiled. "You started it."

He threaded his hands in her hair. "Would you mind very much if we did the not-just-sex stuff one more time before we go to the workshop?"

"You really do want me to sit for you?" she asked.

Right past the bedroom part of his question. Okay, he could deal with that. "Yes. If you don't mind." He held out his hands, studying them. "When you stumbled on me last night I was already in sensory overload. I should have been more considerate, but I'd been thinking of you, of the way you felt, the way you'd kissed me." How could he make her understand? "The feel of marble in my hands—it's smooth. Sensuous." He glanced at her. "I wasn't sure I hadn't dreamed you. I'm still not sure."

"Only one way to find out."

She was flirting again, or at least she sounded like she was. "What way is that?" he asked, hoping like hell it meant modeling could wait half an hour.

"Do it again," she said. "The not-just-sex thing."

He wanted to scoop her up and carry her into his bedroom—like the troglodyte he was. No. She deserved better than the caveman treatment.

"I read your blog," he told her.

Her face transformed from hot and sexy to a look of sheer terror. Maggie backed away. "Oh? I was g-g-going to tell you. I hope you d-d-don't mind."

He stepped closer to her and placed a finger to her lips. "You *are* a 'better person.' I'd be lying if I told you I didn't enjoy what we've shared, but I also don't want you to feel like I'm taking advantage of you."

She blinked. Inhaled deeply. "Why do *I* feel like the one who's taking advantage of *you*?"

"Then let's take advantage of each other, and when we're done, we can go out to the workshop so I can preserve your reputation by finishing your statue."

"Always the hero," she whispered, rocking on her toes to kiss him. "Thank you for your thoughtfulness, but my reputation doesn't need to be preserved." She wrapped her arms around his neck. "I'll keep your secret. I won't let anyone know the confirmed bachelor is still human, with wants..." She nipped his lips. "...and needs." She kissed him again.

To hell with playing the gentleman. "And right now I need you." Thad slid an arm behind her knees, lifted her and carried her to his bed.

Chapter 17

A s Maggie drove past the real estate office on Monday morning, she second-guessed herself one more time. She still hadn't gone in to check their listings. Did she want to stay in Edgarville?

The more time she spent with Thad, the more time she wanted to spend with him. He wasn't a brooding, tragic hero anymore. He was a vital, tantalizing man whom she'd reclassified as the strong, silent type. She didn't dare forget his confirmed bachelor status. Keeping a little distance would be a good idea, and that meant *not* moving to Edgarville, where it was too easy to take advantage of each other at a moment's notice.

She'd hold off on looking for a place to buy for another week, after Torie came to visit. Torie could help her put things into perspective.

The parking lot at the Cascade Building was half full when she arrived. She spotted Jean's car and parked beside it, gathered her tote bag and walked inside. She stopped at the kiosk to reserve a desk before she headed for the elevator.

As the elevator door started to close, a hand reached in, followed by the person it was attached to. Preston. Maggie scowled while he stepped into the elevator.

"If it isn't M-m-m-Maggie," he said, mocking her stutter. "What b-b-brings you into the office t-t-today?"

She refused to stoop to his level. "Same reason you're here," she said clearly, without a hitch.

He turned to face her, narrowing his eyes. "Why aren't you stuttering?"

"You know, sometimes speech disorders resolve themselves," she said. She couldn't say hers had completely resolved, but she was done being intimidated by a bully.

"You seem awfully sure of yourself these days. Do you know something I don't? Last I checked, all our jobs were hanging in the balance, yours and mine most specifically. Aren't you worried?"

Maggie straightened her shoulders. "No point worrying about tomorrow. If I need to find a new job, I'm sure I will."

"Isn't it hard to interview with a s-s-stutter?" he asked, taking a step into her personal space.

She wasn't going to back down.

"P-p-p." She winced. He'd gotten to her again. "The world is less likely to judge my speech than the quality of my work." Most of the time. But he didn't need to know that.

The doors opened, and Maggie relaxed. Next time she'd take the stairs. Preston shouldered past her—what a gentleman—and she headed for the desk she'd reserved.

Jean was seated in the cubicle next to hers. Maggie lowered her voice. "Did you ever make it home last night?"

Jean giggled and turned around. "Late. Very late."

"Does that mean you're going to see him again?"

"Yeah, at least once more, but he was a little overeager. Sort of like a puppy with a new toy. We made a date for next weekend and I'll decide if he's trainable then."

Maggie laughed.

"I didn't mean to shoo you away, you know." Jean made a dramatic pout. "What did you end up doing?"

Maggie's skin tingled. "I managed to find something. Had a very relaxing evening." Bone-melting might be a better description, but as long as Thad wasn't going public with their relationship, she wasn't going to, either. "Didn't get as much reading done as I should have, though."

Sloane stuck her head out of her office and glanced around the cubicles. "Maggie. Haven't seen today's blog post."

"On my computer. Bad internet connection at the place I'm renting here in town so I figured I'd send it once I got into the office."

"I hope it's more of your tragic hero."

Maggie winced, ready to put Haunted Heathcliff behind her with hopes no one would ever know where he'd originated. "I have a book review today. We'd only agreed on a week's worth of my Haunted Heathcliff. I wouldn't want him to get stale." *Please don't make me write more blogs about Thad.*

"I suppose you might have a point. What are you thinking about for tomorrow?"

"I've queued a week's worth of life in a small town," Maggie told her.

Sloane frowned. "I hate this town."

That didn't bode well for her next series of posts. "It has its perks."

"Do you have a moment to step into my office?" Sloane cocked her head and disappeared.

Odd.

"Duh-duh-duh," Jean said, signaling the chords of doom.

Maggie frowned and headed into Sloane's office.

Sloane placed her palms on her desk and looked up. "Close the door."

Maggie took a seat. "Everything okay?"

"That's what I need to ask you." Sloane leaned over her desk. "Several people have commented on Preston Andrews' rude behavior, especially where you're concerned. I've mentioned it to HR, but I wanted to talk to you personally."

Maggie swallowed a bundle of nerves. "I d-d-don't see the point in making a b-b-big deal out of it. I can p-p-put up with him a couple of days a month." She managed a smile. "This is when it helps to work remotely."

Sloane continued to stare at her. "The thing is, if he's harassing you, he's likely harassing other people, as well. It's important to document his behavior to spare other people the..." She looked to the side, in search of the word she wanted to use.

"Humiliation?" Maggie supplied.

Sloane nodded.

"Is this your way of telling me other people have documented similar incidents?"

Again Sloane nodded, then spoke deliberately. "I'm not at liberty to discuss any other information I might or might not have."

"Understood." Maggie drew a deep breath. "Is there someone in HR I should speak to?"

Sloane slid a card across the desk. "Between you and me, in my experience, men like Preston have deep-seated issues. Watch your back, Maggie. I don't trust him."

That made two of them. "Understood."

"How long do you plan to be in the office today?" Sloane tapped a pen on her desk.

"I was planning to leave after the status meeting."

"Good. I'd rather keep you out of the line of fire."

What did Sloane know that Maggie didn't?

Maggie rose from her seat and reached for the door handle. "Thank you. I'll call HR today."

People were filtering into the conference room. Her phone call to HR would have to wait until after the status meeting.

Maggie grabbed a pad of paper and a pen from her desk, tucked her cell phone into her pocket and nearly ran into Preston. Instead of allowing her to pass, he blocked each step she took to go around him.

"Jackhole," she muttered, and raised her eyebrows when she realized she hadn't stuttered. He seemed to notice, too, because he narrowed his eyes.

They walked into the conference room together and he raised his voice enough for the rest of the room to hear. "You ought to find something more original for your blog rather than plagiarizing Miss Brontë's work."

"Not plagiarizing," she replied. "Inspired by."

She took a seat beside Jean, making Preston walk to the other side of the table.

"We'll see what Sloane has to say about it," Preston said. He glanced around the table. "She isn't usually late to a meeting. Anyone know what's going on?"

"Probably fussing that she can't get what she wants in such a small town," one of the feature writers said.

Sloane breezed into the room, closing the door before she made her way to her seat. "Let's get started." She gave Maggie a nod. "Your blog has garnered more hits than any other webpage this last week. Good job, Maggie."

"As long as you don't mind rehashing Wuthering Heights," Preston said.

Sloane speared him with a squint. "Which makes it that much better. Our magazine caters to readers. If she can make a classic relatable in modern day terms, she's done her job. I'm assuming you've read the book? Or at least seen the movie?"

"I have," he said.

"Then I'll assume you're a Cathy hater. You wouldn't be the first man who took offense to her characterization." She turned to Maggie once more. "Looking forward to your next offering.

"Jean. How's your article coming along? I haven't seen a draft yet."

"I'll have it in your email end of day," Jean said. "I'm waiting for CVs from my references."

An hour later, Maggie joined the bustle to exit the conference room. She stopped by her cubicle and turned when Preston cleared his throat. Her skin crawled. "Can I help you?"

"Why aren't you stuttering?" he asked.

"It's something I've worked very hard to overcome," she said with new-found confidence. "Is that a problem?"

"Maybe it's because you have a new boyfriend here in town. Is he your Heathcliff?"

What did Preston know?

"You already know Sloane asked me to invent the episodes on my blog," she said carefully. "Heathcliff belongs to Miss Brontë."

"And that slab of meat who defended you the other day?"

Maggie rose to her feet. What was the point in engaging him in conversation? "If you stopped offending everyone who crosses your path, you might make some friends here, too. Oh. Wait. You don't have any friends. There must be a reason for that."

"They're not your friends," he said with a sneer. "They feel sorry for the poor woman who has trouble speaking."

And yet she hadn't stuttered once since he'd approached her desk. Maggie raised an eyebrow to emphasize her point. She gathered her computer and her books and tucked them into her tote bag.

"If you'll excuse me, I have work to do." Maggie shouldered past Preston. "Have a good day."

Chapter 18

"Here's another one," Amy said, spinning around in her chair.

Thad looked up from the bills stacked on his desk, wondering how much longer he'd be able to pay them. While he didn't wish anyone dead, he did need more work. "Another what?" he asked.

She huffed, hit a button on her keyboard and the printer spit out a sheet of paper. "A work order for a garden statue. That's five today alone. I told you this would be a good idea."

"Five?"

She raised her eyebrows and gave him a look as if he was dense. "I created a new folder for you." She pointed a finger at him. "Hey, maybe Rachel's dog is helping to garner interest. And have you asked the Cemetery Association if you could do a presentation on headstone ornaments yet?"

Thad reached for a paper towel and wiped the perspiration off his forehead. "No."

"What are you waiting for? Someone to do it for you?"

"I've been busy."

"Not here you haven't." She pushed off and her chair wheeled across the floor toward him, a folder in her hand. "How's the new statue coming? Can I see it?"

While he'd spent some of his time with Maggie sculpting, he'd spent more time appreciating the real thing. "Not done yet," he said, taking the folder.

"It's good of her to sit for you." She rolled back to her desk.

Good of her. As if Amy wrote off his relationship to Maggie as a favor. Because why would a woman like Maggie be interested in him?

Why indeed. And yet she seemed to be interested. Unlike Ginny, who'd frequently reminded him he was little more than a tool, Maggie actually made love to him—with her eyes open.

Thad shook his head. *Made love*? She had said it was more than sex, but making love was a fairly big leap. Did he dare to hope he might have something with Maggie that had eluded him all these years? Something he'd missed out on with the other women in his life? Or was he fooling himself?

"You want to quote those requests out?" Amy asked. "From what I've seen of your work, I'm guessing you can get the statues done fairly quickly."

He opened the folder and glanced down. "I have no idea what to charge."

Amy crooked a finger at him and he walked over to her desk. She pointed to her computer screen, where she'd Googled garden statues.

"That's for ceramic," she said. "I'm thinking your stone pieces are more durable and, therefore, you can demand a higher price." She pointed to one of the requests that had come in, a request for a squirrel. "How many hours would this take you? Figure an hourly rate, figure the cost of materials…"

"I get it," he said.

"Do you? What you've done so far hasn't cost you much because you've used scrap. Charge them for the material. Cost plus."

The marble he'd bought to sculpt Maggie had cost him plenty, but Amy didn't need to know that. He wiped a hand over his mouth, staring at Amy's search results, then at Amy. Despite his reluctance to take on her idea, it was delivering results. "Thank you."

Her back straightened and her eyes grew wide. "For what?"

"Helping me save the family business." Those five orders would keep him busy the rest of the week, assuming no one died for a couple of days, and they'd pay some of the bills. "Don't suppose you'd like to take a first run at that presentation you want me to give. After all, you don't have any other work to do while things are slow, and I, on the other hand, have statues to carve."

"I'll even call and see if you can get a spot on the agenda." She smacked him on the butt. "Meanwhile, you need to put together quotes for these requests."

"I can handle that."

"But I want to see them first."

He narrowed his eyes at her.

"I have a stake in this business, too," she said. "I want to make sure you're giving them—and us—fair consideration."

He thumbed through the sheets in the folder. A bird, a lion, a little girl beside a flower pot, a fairy with wings, and a squirrel. He calculated size, figuring the tallest of them would only be a foot or two in height. Thad headed into the shop behind the showroom and assessed the scraps he had on hand. The bird and the squirrel would be easy enough. He'd have to order material for the other three.

And then there was his statue of Maggie. When would he have time to work on that?

With a slow smile, he figured the longer he took finishing that project, the more time he could spend with Maggie. If Amy's assessment was right and Maggie was merely doing him a favor, he didn't mind taking his time. As long as Maggie was willing to hang around a while.

Chapter 19

T he rain had started on Tuesday, and after being holed away in her rental all week, when the sun came out again on Thursday, Maggie was itchy to get outside to read.

The *Reading Women* blog was on autopilot, and while her "small town life" observations—complete with comparisons to novels that took place in small towns—was doing well, web page visits and comments were down. Maybe inspiration would hit her if she went for a walk along Main Street.

Maybe she'd run into Thad Benson.

He'd called her every night, but he'd also been busy all week with an influx of orders and, like her, he was focused on earning his paycheck. Maggie was getting antsy to see him—to touch him—and Torie was coming for a weekend visit. If she didn't run into him today, it would be Sunday night or Monday again before they could "take advantage of cach other."

He hadn't invited her over. If he wanted time with her, he would have suggested it, wouldn't he? Then again, he was a confirmed bachelor.

If he wanted her there, he'd have asked.

She headed to the cemetery, not because it was a quiet place where she wouldn't be disturbed. No, this time she went hoping to catch a glimpse of Thad.

She was in worse shape than she thought if she was plotting ways to accidentally run into him.

Instead of stopping, Maggie continued past the cemetery gate, past the monument shop. At the end of the block, she found a parking lot marked for people using the local bike trail. A nice long walk would get rid of her extra energy. She'd find a place in the shade along the trail where she could sit for a while and read.

Tote bag in hand, she started down the gravel path that wound around knolls and through a canopy of trees. A cool breeze fluttered through her hair, and when she emerged into sunlight again, it warmed her face.

Edgarville wasn't such a bad little town. There were attractions other than the giant of a man who'd given her a more-than-warm welcome. She'd made new friends. She could buy a bike and ride the trail. And on those nights when Thad decided he needed company, she could warm his bed.

Was that enough? Wasn't that the equivalent of offering herself as the proverbial blow-up doll?

A dirt path veered away from the gravel, marked with a sign that read "creek." A creek certainly sounded like a peaceful place to sit with a book. She followed the path and within moments heard the sounds of rushing water. As she turned a bend, the trees thinned out. Sunlight dappled the advertised creek as it tripped over rocks. A slope of tall grass waved in the wind, and two weather-worn park benches waited beside the water.

Maggie raised her face to the sun and smiled. She'd found her spot. Peaceful. Quiet. Out of the way. No one would bother her here. She reached into her tote for one of the books, swept the skirt of her sundress out of the way and sat on the bench.

The book was one of the better ones she'd read in a while, a historical romance featuring a reluctant duke and the bluestocking he was in love with, forbidden fruit. She'd reached the part in the book where, try as he might, the duke couldn't seem to keep his hands off the virginal heroine. Not that the virginal heroine was complaining. She was doing her best to encourage his advances, as much out of curiosity of the intimacies between men and women as for her attraction to the duke.

Maggie rested a hand over her heart, engrossed in the scene unfolding on the page. *Well done, author.* Her body thrummed in response to what she was reading, so much so that she imagined for a moment she heard Thad's voice calling out to her.

If only.

She closed her eyes, picturing the scene, and she could almost smell Thad. The earthy stone scent she'd come to associate with him, along with something much earthier, the muskiness of his glistening skin, like Lady Chatterley's woodsman. She imagined his breath on her neck.

"That sounds like fun."

His deep voice startled her. She banged her head against his jaw.

Thad was reading over her shoulder.

"I've missed you this week," he said, his voice rumbling through her like thunder.

Maggie melted against him and closed her eyes once more. "I missed you, too," she whispered.

139

Thad sat beside her on the bench, and bent to kiss the sensitive skin of her neck.

No sense pretending she wasn't primed and ready. "Where can we go?" she said with a gasp.

"Right here." He slid his hands under her skirt and tugged her panties down. "On the ground or on the bench?"

She fumbled with his belt, his zipper, and when he sprang free, she kicked a leg over and sat on his lap. How had she gone all week without this man?

He buried his face in her chest, nipping and licking and kissing while she rode him. She stared into his eyes, watching his passion burning bright, sharing her own. Could he see how much she'd come to care for him? How much she wanted this to go on and on? She clutched his shoulders, felt the cords of muscle tighten under her fingers right before he squeezed his eyes closed and grunted, pushing deep inside.

God, he felt good.

And then he shrank away.

She wasn't done. She wanted more.

As if he knew, he eased her off his lap, set her on the edge of the bench and reached between her legs, stroking her gently, taking her the rest of the way home.

"I love it when you scream my name," he whispered in her ear. "Come over tonight?"

Panting, she tugged his shirt, bringing him close until she had enough breath to kiss him. The man could kiss like no one else. She came up for air and looked into his eyes, that luminescent shade of amber. "What time?"

"Is now too soon?"

Maggie giggled and he grinned.

"Dinner," he said. "Six o'clock. No. That's too late. Five o'clock for appetizers in the bedroom before we eat, and then we can eat at six. Unless the appetizers become too distracting, in which case we'll eat when we're too weak to go on."

"The appetizers are already distracting," she said. And then she realized where they were. "Oh." She looked around and straightened her dress. "What if somebody saw us?"

"Want to give them another show?" he asked with a mischievous grin.

A lurch in her abdomen responded. She nipped at his lips once more, tempted to move under cover of the tall grass.

"Although they're going to think someone's killing you if they hear you screaming like that again." He stroked her hair.

"I didn't scream," she said, pulling back.

"You did. And I intend to make you scream again." He kissed her. "And again." Another kiss. "And again."

"Now?" she asked, practically panting.

"Tonight."

"Promises, promises," she teased.

"I'd promise you anything," he whispered.

Her heart kicked. *Promise me forever?*

He was a confirmed bachelor. She didn't dare ask him for things he couldn't give her, even if that's what she wanted.

"How did you know I'd be here today?" she asked, reaching for her panties.

He cocked his head toward the hill. "The cemetery's up there. I come down to relax beside the water sometimes. It calms my mind."

A flattened path of grass, interspersed with black-eyed susans and lupines, marked the trail he'd made. From where she'd been sitting, a patch of northern sea oats obstructed her view of the top of the hill. No wonder she hadn't seen him coming. "Something bothering you?" she asked.

He smiled. "Not anymore. Pretty sure you just made everything right in my world."

Maggie wanted to sigh, but she didn't dare. Thad wouldn't want a profession of love from her. She closed her eyes again and turned away, struck by the realization that she was, in fact, in love with Thad Benson.

"Bet you say that to all the girls," she teased, trying to lighten the mood.

"Only the ones brave enough to see me naked."

Maggie laughed. "Not nearly naked enough."

Thad tucked himself in and refastened his pants. "Gotta get back to work. Five o'clock?"

"I'll be there."

He leaned over and kissed her. "And if you decide to dress the way you did the first time I invited you over, I wouldn't object."

"You're referring to later? After you made me pay for spying on you in your workshop?"

"You said you didn't mind."

"I came back, didn't I?"

He gave her another crooked grin. "You're a lot warmer than marble."

"Smooth talker. Keep it up and you might not make it back to work."

Thad gave her one more kiss. "Don't tempt me, woman. I'll see you tonight."

He took long strides up the hill, through the tall grass, until he disappeared over the ridge.

Another night of hot sex. One more night of plotless erotica before Torie helped her remember life didn't work out like a romance novel.

Chapter 20

The fairy wings were a challenge.

Thad poked gingerly, attempting a lace-like texture. He should have charged more for this one with the additional detail work. A trickle of sweat burned his eyes and he backed away, reaching for his towel. He shouldn't be sweating this much in the middle of the night.

He shot a glance at the carving he'd done of Ginny's face, one of his first works. He'd captured her perfectly, the mocking expression in her eyes, the hint of a smile.

They'd spent lots of time in the tall grass beside the creek, and he'd asked her more than once to go on a "real" date.

Then the ugly guys will all think they stand a chance.

He seemed to be thinking about Ginny a lot lately. His latest encounter beside the creek apparently stoked his memories.

Maggie made him feel young and virile. So why wasn't he lying beside her right now instead of detailing a fairy's wings? The easy answer was because he didn't want to disturb her sleep.

With the family business hanging in the balance, he certainly had reason to be preoccupied. The garden statues were a godsend for nights like this when he found himself wide awake instead of sleeping.

And then there was the bust of Helena, the angel of mercy who couldn't bring herself to love him. The relief of Danae, who'd left him for a better-looking model.

Thad shook his head to clear the nostalgia. Maggie was different.

Wasn't she?

He scoffed at himself. He'd outgrown thoughts of marriage, of finding a woman who would stand by him.

Hadn't he?

A sheet covered the unfinished statue of Maggie. At five feet tall, it was his most ambitious endeavor. The clay model depicted her in one of her sundresses, sitting on a tree stump and reading a book. Her face was recognizable in the marble, and he'd carved parts of the tree stump, had pared away sections of her core, but this sculpture was different.

With one hand on the sheet, he considered taking a break from the fairy and moving to what he considered would be his masterpiece.

He could never do justice to Maggie. She was so much more than a beautiful face.

Instead, Thad wiped his face with the towel one more time. The lack of sleep was making him maudlin. That had to be the answer to why he was so nostalgic, why his pulse quickened with every thought of Maggie.

Why he thought he might be in love with Maggie.

Thad let out a slow breath and plopped onto his stool in front of the fairy.

Thank heaven for garden statues.

Time to get his head out of his ass and get the job done. He returned to work on the wings, chipping, sanding, scraping, refining, losing himself in the trance of the work.

Did he smell coffee? What time was it?

Thad shook his head and glanced at the window, at the sun streaming through. He stood, rested his hands at the small of his back and tilted backward to a series of crackles up his spine. He turned to find Maggie leaning against the doorframe wearing one of his shirts, watching him, a cup of coffee in hand.

A vision.

"You want a cup?" she asked.

His heart skipped. "Yeah, that'd be nice."

She disappeared into the house and returned moments later with a second cup.

He took the cup from her and leaned down to kiss her. "Thank you."

"Trouble sleeping?" she asked.

"Trying to get these orders filled so I have the weekend free. Can you come back tonight? Stay the weekend?"

Her expression turned apologetic, her smile wistful. "No, my sister's coming for a visit."

Couldn't be an excuse. It would be too easy to disprove. "Did you tell me your family lives in Indiana?"

"Torie owns a duplex in Foxfield. She and I were roommates until I moved here, but yeah, my mom and dad live in Indiana."

He took a sip of his coffee. Double cream, the way he liked it. She must have seen Sandra prepare it at the café. "Did you tell me you grew up there? Indiana?"

"Yep. Moved to Illinois when I got the job with *Reading Women*." She smiled. "I'd ask you about your family, but I've heard the four generations thing. Sounds like you've lived here all your life."

"And you've also met my siblings. Don't think you've met my folks, yet. If you hang around town long enough, you're bound to run into them, too. My mom's at the monument shop all the time. She hasn't gotten the hang of retirement. She claims she stops in to see Amy's kids, but that's an excuse."

"And your dad?"

"Bowling, fishing, the Lodge. He keeps pretty busy. He's loving not having to go to work anymore." Thad took another sip of coffee. "What time is it?"

"A little after seven. Did you get any sleep?"

"Some." He set his mug down and wrapped his arms around her. "Maybe we should go back to bed."

She chuckled. "I'm good with that, but my hours are more flexible. Don't you have to show up at the monument shop?"

"Not until nine."

"Which only gives you an hour and a half to catch up on your sleep."

Sleep. She'd skipped right over the other things they might do in bed. Intentionally?

He owed her more than time in his bedroom. "I'd like to meet your sister. How about if I take you both to dinner at Riccardo's tonight."

She swallowed hard. "Don't you meet your brothers at Murphy's on Fridays? At least that's what Sandra says. We could bump into each other there."

Did she not want to be seen with him in public? She was suggesting a casual encounter people might not pay attention to, and for some reason, that pissed him off. It was time people knew she was more than his model.

What was she?

Now wasn't the time to analyze their relationship.

"I'll see you there," he said.

She nodded.

He'd take what he could get.

Chapter 21

As Maggie walked her sister down Main Street, she pointed out the two blocks of local businesses from Riccardo's, the nice Italian restaurant, to the trophy shop. She explained how she hadn't had time—a little white lie—to stop into the real estate office for more permanent housing.

She went on to tell Torie about Preston's latest harassment and Sloane's suggestion to report it to HR.

Maggie didn't stutter once, not even to her own hearing.

"I'm so glad you're here," she said by the time they'd reached Murphy's.

Torie laughed. "I can tell. I missed you, too."

They walked inside and Delia greeted her. She skipped her "menus on the table" spiel when she recognized Maggie. Instead, she said, "Nice to see you again. Where's your other friend?"

"I think she went home tonight," Maggie said.

Delia sighed. "Oh, well." She cast a glance at the table where Brian Benson sat sulking, shook her head, and bustled to the bar.

Maggie grabbed Torie's hand and pulled her to an open booth.

"So why does she look disappointed?" Torie asked. "Does she have a thing for your other friend?"

"No, her former boyfriend has a thing for my other friend, the boyfriend she wants to ditch."

Torie laughed, and then put a hand to her mouth when Delia appeared tableside.

"Truth," Delia said, confirming she'd overheard the conversation. "Now. What can I get you ladies?"

"No secrets in a small town," Maggie said.

"Also truth," Delia said with a smile.

"Glass of Chardonnay," Torie ordered.

"Two," Maggie added, and then leaned across the table when Delia walked away. "So why aren't you at the Scott Michaels concert tonight? You could have taken that guy you've been seeing."

"It's our thing, Mags. Yours and mine. Not to mention I'm currently between boyfriends, myself."

"Didn't work out? Oh, honey. I really thought…" she waved off the notion. "I'm sure that won't last long. I swear, they line up behind you like bees to honey. So what's going on at work these days?"

Torie went on to tell her about her office gossip, stopping only when Delia arrived with their drinks.

"Dinner, ladies?" Delia asked.

"I need a minute," Torie said.

Delia grinned. "Back in a few."

Maggie knew the moment Thad walked in. Her skin tingled and she considered, for half a second, how mad her sister would be if Maggie left her alone at the rental tonight. Torie wouldn't miss her while she was sleeping, after all. Then she gave herself a mental kick.

Garth trailed behind Thad and the two of them sprawled into the empty chairs at Brian's table.

"Mags?" Torie said. "The grilled chicken?"

"Hmm?" She snapped to attention. "Oh. It's good. They use a really good Italian marinade. And get onion strings on the side." Maggie gave her the thumbs up.

"You're blushing," Torie said.

Maggie raised her eyebrows, posing an unspoken question.

Torie lowered her menu and did a casual scan of the bar. "I'm guessing the guy you were telling me about is here. Your Haunted Heathcliff."

Maggie nodded.

"The hot one at the bar?" she asked.

Maggie checked the bar. Half a dozen locals. And Preston. Her skin immediately crawled. "Which hot one?" she asked.

"Dark hair, button-down shirt, dress pants that show off his backside."

"That, sister dear, is Preston Andrews."

"The jackal you work with?"

"That's pronounced jackhole. Like asswipe. Poo sucker."

Torie laughed. "Someone's going to think you have an anal fixation."

"Only where he's concerned."

Torie checked him once more. "Shame. He's awful easy on the eyes."

"Not after you get to know him, he isn't."

"All right, then where is your Heathcliff?"

Rapidly approaching. Maggie took a fortifying sip of wine. "Incoming."

"Maggie," he said.

"Thad."

"And you must be her sister."

Torie gave Maggie an are-you-kidding-me look. "Torie Grant," she said, holding out her hand.

"Nice to meet you," he said. "Would you ladies care to join us?"

"We wouldn't want to intrude on your brother bonding time," Maggie said.

Thad narrowed his eyes. "If you change your mind…"

"Thanks," she said.

"Talk to you later, then." He tipped two fingers to his forehead and walked away.

Torie immediately leaned across the table and lowered her voice. "Him?"

Maggie nodded.

"I guess it sort of follows the whole Heathcliff thing. You've always had a tendency to see men as heroes out of novels in the early stages of a relationship."

Maggie's spine straightened. "What does that mean?"

Torie scanned the bar once more. "We'll talk more later. Small town, and all. The waitress has already overheard us badmouthing her boyfriend."

"Ex-boyfriend," Delia said, appearing beside the table once more. "Ready to order?"

Two hours later, they sat in Maggie's living room in their pajamas and bunny slippers, sharing another bottle of wine and laughing the way only sisters could.

Maggie closed her eyes and melted into the easy chair.

"Okay," Torie said. "True confessions time. I want to know what you see in this Heathcliff guy. He must be good in bed, because I have to be honest with you. He's not the most attractive man in the world."

Maggie gave way to a lazy smile. "Yeah, he's good in bed." Then she opened her eyes. "Wait a minute. He isn't ugly."

Torie cocked an eyebrow over the top of her wineglass. "I didn't think Laurence Olivier was that hot, either. Don't know why women used to swoon over him. Even in the remakes, the actors who portrayed Heathcliff weren't all that swoon-worthy."

"He's a good man," Maggie said.

"Right. You'd mentioned that. Mr. Do-Gooder, but is Mr. Do-Gooder good enough?"

"He isn't Heathcliff," Maggie said. And yet the dead girl continued to haunt him—to haunt her. What was it between Thad and Virginia Carter? "Switching gears. He has a real gift as a sculptor. The way he touches the granite, it's like a religious experience to him."

"That actually sounds creepy, Mags."

"You should see the beautiful work he does." The effects of the wine swirled with her thoughts, combining the things she'd seen in his workshop. "He did a stone carving of the dead girl. It's amazing. And there's a bust of another woman. And a raised portrait. What do you call those? A relief? Did I tell you he's making a statue of me?"

"You did." Torie set her glass on an end table and leaned over her knees. "I can see where the statue is a form of flattery, but I'm still going with creepy. The way he collects his women in stone? Like you're part of his collection. Forget Heathcliff. I'm picturing Svengali and he has you snookered."

"No." Maggie shook her head and her eyeballs rattled. She might have had one glass too many of wine. "He cares about his family. Sings songs with his niece. Plays with his nephew. The family business is in danger of going under, but his sister is putting together a portfolio for him. His sister-in-law is helping him market his art. She's pretty sure he can make a mint selling his garden statues. He made a beautiful dog. It looked so real you'd want to pet it." She frowned, remembering Amy's insults. "His sister doesn't seem to see him as human."

"Huh?"

Maggie huffed. "We're living in small town America here. I was at his house until the wee hours of the morning—people knew I'd been there—and the next morning when it looked as if he hadn't gone to bed, they didn't even whisper innuendos."

"Do you go on dates?"

"We've been to dinner."

"Is he attentive when you go out? Demonstrative? Holding hands? Arm around your waist? A kiss now and then?"

Maggie met Torie's insistent stare, but blinked several times. "He hugged me after our first date. In the alley beside the restaurant." She grinned in recollection. "That's when I kissed him."

Torie cocked an eyebrow again. "In the alley?"

When Maggie didn't respond, Torie continued. "If he doesn't show his interest in public, why would anyone think differently? Maggie, I can tell by the way you're defending him that you're more involved than you think you are. I have a hunch this isn't going to end well."

Maggie scoffed. "I'm just having a little fun."

"No, he's having a little fun. You're trying to save him. He's a misfit. Like you envision yourself to be—and you're not, by the way. I'm guessing you're much more comfortable with yourself than he is with himself. A man like that should be excited to show off a pretty girlfriend instead of keeping it on the down-low."

"It's a small town," Maggie said weakly.

"Those brothers of his? They're good looking men, but the one you got?" Torie shook her head. "Something doesn't add up, Mags."

"He's a confirmed bachelor. He isn't looking for a girlfriend."

"Just a hook-up," Torie said.

"What if I'm the one looking for a hook-up? I kissed him first."

Torie reached for Maggie's hand. "You deserve more than a hook-up. You deserve that storybook hero you're always looking for. The man who steps off the page and into your life."

Maggie chuffed. "Those guys aren't real. Thad Benson is as real as they come."

"Real ugly," Torie said.

"Hey. His face is interesting." She sat back and folded her arms. "Beauty is in the eye of the beholder. You thought Preston Andrews was a stud. It isn't about appearance, Torie. A man's looks—his worth—come from inside."

"You have such a big heart, Maggie. That's the only thing I can figure for how you can still believe in love. I hope, for your sake, this guy's worth it." Torie made a pouty puppy face that aggravated Maggie.

"We're just having fun," Maggie repeated.

"I know you better than that. And you know what else? He's one lucky S.O.B." Torie left her chair to sit beside Maggie on the couch. "You should invite him to Mom's for the Fourth of July."

Maggie held her hands up. "Hang on. That's a little drastic, don't you think? Meet the parents?"

"And Lacey," she said. "Oh. Maybe that's not such a good idea. Probably should have thought that through."

Except now that Torie had said something, she'd made Maggie consider what other people would think.

Living with a stutter had taught her not to care what other people thought. "What do you have against my Haunted Heathcliff?" Maggie asked.

Torie smirked. "You're not really sleeping with him, are you? I get that you moved out to give me space, but if you're going to make up a boyfriend, you might have picked someone more attractive. Even that jackhole at the bar."

"You think I'm lying?" Maggie sputtered.

"Aren't you the one who's always telling me not to turn into an old maid like you? Maggie, I like being single, and I'm pretty sure you do, too. So what if we never get married?"

Maggie rose to her feet. "You think I invented a relationship?" she asked once more. She glanced at the door, wondering if it was too late for that booty call.

Torie held up a palm. "Okay, okay. I'm sorry. I don't see it, but I believe you. Okay? I'm just saying, Lacey would have a field day with him."

"Lacey's a spoiled brat," Maggie pointed out. "Self-centered, immature, blamestormer. Mean. I expected better from you."

"Lacey's my sister, too, you know. For better or worse, we're stuck with her."

Maggie covered her eyes with a hand, struggling to calm her temper. "She never made fun of *you*."

"We're all grown up now," Torie said, taking a defensive tone.

"That hasn't stopped her from being mean. Why do you think she never calls me?"

"Because you struggle on the phone?" Torie suggested.

"Not with people I'm comfortable around. But I guess that excludes her, doesn't it?"

"Can't you put the past behind?" Torie tugged at Maggie's hand to get her to sit, but Maggie yanked free.

"Not when every other word she speaks to me is a passive-aggressive barb," Maggie said.

Torie heaved a dramatic sigh. "You know she thinks you're the spoiled one, don't you?"

"So I've heard, although I'm not sure how she arrived at that conclusion. And I suppose that makes you the tortured middle child?"

"Let's not go there," Torie said. "I'm sorry I said anything. If you want to date Cyrano de Bergerac, that's up to you."

"He is not..." Maggie closed her eyes. "I'm going to bed."

Torie heaved another sigh. "I'm sorry. Don't be mad at me."

"Why would you care if I'm mad at you? If you cared about my feelings, you wouldn't be making fun of the man I love."

Torie's eyes grew round. She set her drink down. "Come again?"

157

Maggie covered her mouth with her hand. She'd actually said it out loud.

"You're in love with your Haunted Heathcliff?" Torie asked.

Maggie shook her head. "You know... I don't know for sure, but he's a good man, and he deserves better than insults. Especially from my family."

Torie rose to her feet. "You sure he isn't another romantic ideal? You do have a tendency to compare your men to fictional heroes. Remember your Mr. Darcy boyfriend?"

Maggie shoulders slumped. "He stopped being Heathcliff a long time ago."

"And the dead girl? His Catherine?"

"I don't know." Maggie's throat swelled as she struggled to swallow her emotions.

Torie hugged her. "I'm sorry, Mags. I won't say another mean thing about him, I promise. If I'd have known..." She stepped back. "You really are leaving me to be an old maid by myself, aren't you?"

Maggie laughed, dislodging a tear from her eye. "You said you like being single."

"I do. For now. But who knows? That could change. Clearly, it did for you."

"Still not sure I can compete with a ghost," Maggie said.

"He can't sleep with a ghost."

There was that blow-up doll image again. "But he can pretend." Was that enough?

"You're going to make me say something mean about him again," Torie teased.

"We could go back to making fun of Lacey," Maggie joked.

"I know you better than that." Torie retrieved her wine glass and took another drink. "As I recall, you were the first one she called when her marriage fell apart."

"To blame me," Maggie said.

"And you let her, even though you both knew better. We're sisters, after all."

"Can't pick your family," Maggie said.

"I'd pick you every time."

Maggie chuckled. "You'll have to check back with me tomorrow if you're expecting me to say the same."

Torie laughed. "I deserve that."

Maggie exhaled a dramatic sigh. "Hey, if my own sister can't tell me the truth, who can? At least I know what the rest of the world is thinking now, even if I don't happen to agree with them."

She managed a smile and nudged Torie. "Yeah, I'd pick you, too."

Chapter 22

O rders for garden statues continued to come in every day from all over the country. Whatever magic Sandra had done with the Benson Monuments website was working. At the rate they were going, Thad had enough work to keep him busy into the slow, winter months.

As he sorted through the scrap behind the monument shop, he mentally calculated raw material needs for the orders in-hand.

"Thad," Amy called from the showroom. "You need to look at this presentation and tell me if it's okay."

The Cemetery Association presentation. He owed Amy for looking out for him and the family business. He'd considered a rendering of the two kids—Chloe and Randall—on a park bench, but he'd already made the leprechaun for their garden when she married Kevin. She didn't need another lawn ornament, even though a statue of the two kids appealed to him.

"Thad!" Amy yelled.

"I'm coming." He glanced at her computer screen as he walked into the showroom.

A slideshow ran, showing pictures of the headstone ornaments he'd done.

She looked at him over her shoulder. "I got to thinking if I can get pictures of you making one of these in various stages to run in the background while you do your sales pitch, shoot a quick video of you carving something…"

"Sales pitch?"

She huffed. "That's the point, Thad. You're pitching the funeral directors to up-sell. Why do people put these on their headstones? It's about personal touch, and that's what Benson Monuments represents. Do I have to do all the work for you?"

He blinked at Amy. She was particularly short-tempered today. Kevin had returned from New York. He usually left her dreamy-eyed, especially after they'd been apart for a few days.

"Something wrong?" Thad asked.

"Why do I even try," she said, pushing away from her desk. "I'm going to the cemetery."

Thad wrote her mood off to a lover's quarrel and sat in front of her computer. He flipped through the slides she'd prepared, along with speaker notes. She'd done a good job, but it was his presentation. He needed to step up and do his part.

While Thad added notes of his own, Brian wandered in.

"You're late," Thad said.

"For what? We suddenly have a rush on headstones?" Brian plopped into the desk chair opposite and leaned back.

Must be something in the air that two of his siblings were in such unpleasant moods today. Thad folded his arms and swung his chair around to face Brian. "Something particular on your mind?"

Brian glared at him a moment before he straightened. "Been offered a job."

One less employee on the payroll.

One less set of hands in the cemetery to mount stones.

"Go on."

"At the college, when I graduated—they have counselors who steer you into your field."

"Yeah…"

"A chance like this doesn't come along every day. In fact, hardly ever."

Thad massaged his forehead. "Straight up, Brian. What's the job?"

He leaned over his knees, his eyes alight with an excitement Thad hadn't seen since they were kids. "The Haley Estate in Widdersfield is looking for a horticulturist, someone to oversee the gardens and maintain the golf course."

Widdersfield. A hundred miles away. "That's great," he said, wondering if that meant he might still call on Brian to help from time to time, and yet he didn't want to dictate Brian's future. Thad had figured his little brother would be a professional student. Brian had been searching for majors for six years before he finally settled on Horticulture. "When do they want you to start?"

"I know summer's our busy time. I didn't want to leave you high and dry." Brian looked nervous. "They asked me to start first of July. It's their busy time, too. It's a once in a lifetime chance."

Thad rose to his feet and extended a hand. "Congrats. Gonna miss you around here."

Brian jumped to his feet and pulled Thad into a hug. Was he crying?

"If you need me, I'm only a phone call away," he said, swiping at his eyes.

"I will, but I'll try not to," Thad said. His own eyes stung, but he refused to acknowledge the knot in his chest.

Brian cleared his throat and turned away. "Anything going on here today?"

More than Thad wanted to deal with. "If you wouldn't mind watching the shop for a few minutes. Amy went out to the cemetery and I need a little fresh air myself."

"You got it."

Thad gave him a nod and walked out the front door. He headed down the road without a destination in mind.

When they'd been kids, their uncles were always around the shop, sandblasting or carving headstones. His Uncle Julian had been the one who'd taught Thad his hand-carving techniques.

Garth had his own place now, and with Brian leaving, the only family left to run Benson Monuments was Thad and Amy.

Was he a dinosaur? Garth had moved ahead with the times with his engraving business. Fewer people wanted headstones, and those who did were looking for more modern techniques, like laser etching pictures rather than stone carvings. Benson Monuments didn't have the capital to invest in that kind of equipment. If he sold the business, would he be letting the family down?

What was he going to do?

He needed a walk beside the creek to get his thoughts in order.

First Amy, then Garth, and now Brian. They were all still there, all still family, but one by one they'd moved on to live their own lives. Even his parents had retired. Where once the whole family had worked together all day, every day, now they had to schedule times to be together.

And where was his life? He might like to think things would have worked out with Ginny if she hadn't died, but he knew better.

When he'd met Helena at the hospital, she'd been kind-hearted and comforting, but she'd made it clear she wasn't interested in pursuing anything more. And then there was Danae. He'd thought she was the one.

No. He might have wanted to marry her, but even he knew that was desperation more than love. The prize went to her for sticking around longer than the rest, but even she'd run off.

He trotted down the hill, through the tall grass and stopped to lean against a tree trunk. Allowing himself a moment of self-pity, tears cooled the sting behind his eyes. He hastily wiped them with the back of his hands.

He stormed on, his emotions running high. If he sat by the edge of the creek, took his shoes off and cooled his feet, maybe he'd feel better. He listened to the water, rounded a bend in the trail and his heart stopped beating.

Maggie.

He wasn't desperate anymore. He'd wanted to propose to Danae to keep her from leaving him, but that wasn't the answer. Looking back, he knew that better now than he did then. What he felt for Danae was... nothing like what he felt for Maggie.

She was half-hidden in the tall grass, sitting on a blanket and reading a book, but this time, she'd seen him coming. Maggie set her book down and smiled at him. When she did that, all was right with the world.

"Hey, big guy," she said.

The same way Sandra greeted Garth, and Thad's insides turned to mush. Sandra loved Garth, after all. It was obvious with every look she gave him. Every smile. Every word.

"Hey, yourself," he said, not daring to hope.

"Didn't you come over the hill last time?" she asked.

"I did."

She held out a hand for him to join her on the ground, but as he drew closer, her smile drooped. "Something wrong?"

He sat beside her, pulled her close, breathed in her scent, nuzzled the curls that tickled his nose. "Not anymore." He held her for what felt like an eternity before he eased away.

Maggie looked into his eyes and brushed a stray tear from his cheek.

"Hay fever," he said.

"Liar." She grinned at him.

He wanted what Amy had. What Garth had. With this woman. "I want to go public," he said.

Those great big eyes grew larger. "With?"

"You and me. Screw the gossips. I want people to know we're a thing. Dating. Having 'more than sex.'" His heart hiccupped, waiting for her response.

She laughed. Laughter was scary.

"The confirmed bachelor?" she said. "Aren't you afraid I'll taint your reputation?"

"I'm not scared if you're not," he said.

A pained look crossed her expression. "Why?"

A perfect opening. He loved her. Easy enough to say, but she'd laughed. Would she tell him she was too embarrassed to be seen in public with him? Tell him they'd only been having fun—that she was someone else's loving partner?

"I'm not too good at expressing myself," he said, his voice abandoning him.

"I disagree. I've seen your work, you know. I've been in your man-cave workshop." The pulse at her neck quickened and her nostrils flared. "I've seen the stone carvings."

"Then you know why no one else has seen them," he said.

Why did she look like she was about to cry? "Maggie?"

She rolled her eyes and sighed. "Oh, c'mon. You said you'd read my blog."

He had. She was a romantic. What was he missing? "Right…" Was she waiting for a grand gesture? He pictured Ginny lying in the tall grass, ten feet away, laughing at him. He'd made the mistake of telling Ginny he'd loved her, and she'd told him if he wanted her to continue to take these walks with him by the creek, he'd better get those thoughts out of his head. But she wasn't… "Listen, Ginny…"

Maggie pulled away.

Idiot. Thad shook his head. "Maggie."

She folded her arms.

"Maggie," he said more gently.

166

More tears slid down her cheeks. He'd made a muck of things yet again. Thad pulled her into his arms and held her close.

He kissed her tenderly and tucked a stray curl behind her ear. Maggie's eyes, those beautiful big eyes, watched him silently. "Talk to me," he whispered.

Another voice called from the top of the hill. Amy's. "Thad?"

"She won't see you," he whispered to Maggie. He pushed to his feet, adjusted himself, then started up the hill.

"What are you doing?" Amy asked. "Who are you with?"

Thad looked over his shoulder. While it was obvious someone was there, a patch of sea oats hid Maggie from Amy. If she wanted to go public, this would be the time for her to pop up and say something.

She didn't.

"Flashback," Amy said, a note of panic in her voice.

He steered Amy away, trying to guard Maggie's privacy. "What are you talking about?"

"Oh my God. Thad. I can't un-see what I've just seen. Worse, this isn't the first time I've seen you, except the last time I was just a kid and I didn't know what it was I'd seen." She turned her back on him, but didn't walk away. "Flashback."

He didn't have enough patience for this today. "What are you talking about?"

"You and Ginny. Shit. I remember you and Ginny, but I was a kid and I had no idea why you were all over her then." She poked a finger to her chest. "I have two kids now." She pointed to where Maggie remained hidden in the grass. "How can you not tell me, your sister, that you have a girlfriend? Someone you care enough about to sleep with?"

"Because it's none of your business?" He checked his clothes. Fully dressed. He'd kissed Maggie, cradled her face. He might have thought about doing other things, but Amy had *not* stumbled on a compromising situation. "I don't know what you think you saw…"

"It is my business. All three of you sheltered me from any chance at making friends or having a date while I was growing up. Was that your business?" That pointing finger hit his chest. "You are absolutely my business. How could you keep this from me? Wait. Unless you paid her. Thad, please tell me you didn't pay that woman to sleep with you."

He was done with today. Thad grabbed her finger and leaned into her. "You mean because no woman in their right mind would want to be seen with a troglodyte like me?"

Amy took a step back. "That's not what I meant. I know everything that happens in this tiny town. How can I not know you're seeing someone?"

Except she did know. She just didn't believe it. No wonder Maggie didn't want to go public. They'd all figure he was her pity fuck. "That's what you think of me?" he said, his voice hoarse. "The only way I can get a woman to sleep with me is to pay her?"

"That's not what I meant."

"That's what you said. How many hookers do you know in Edgarville, Amy?"

"Well, Ginny was the next best thing, wasn't she?"

He glared at her and she had the good grace to look ashamed.

168

Kevin crossed through the cemetery. "What are you two arguing about? I can hear you from the street."

Tears ran down Amy's cheeks. Good. She should be sorry for what she'd said. "Take her home, Kevin, before she says anything that might *really* hurt."

Kevin looped an arm over her shoulder. "Amy, what did you say?"

She broke away, crossing her arms.

Kevin extended an arm toward Thad. "There's an explanation."

"I'm sure there is. I'm not sure I want to hear it."

"Don't you dare," Amy sobbed, fixing her glare on Kevin.

"He's your brother. He deserves to know," Kevin said gently.

Tears continued to roll down her face. "Fine. But don't you dare try to blame this on hormones."

The dots connected. Thad closed his eyes and grabbed his forehead. "I get it. You don't have to tell me." He took a step closer to Amy, into her personal space, and looked down at her. She studied her toes. "Being pregnant might make you emotional, as we've all seen, but that doesn't excuse the things you said."

"Twins," Kevin said sheepishly. "So twice as bad."

Thad glanced at Kevin. "Not good enough." He looked down the hill once more, to the indentation in the grass. Maggie had gone.

It was time for him to leave, too.

Chapter 23

For someone who wanted to go public, Thad had a funny way of showing it.

Had he really called her Ginny?

Maggie stormed down the path, under the canopy of trees, fury half-blinding her. What did she expect? He'd suddenly profess his undying love for her? Confirmed bachelors didn't fall in love, *and* he'd called her Ginny. She was back to blow-up doll status.

Who are you with?

They'd both been fully dressed. Not only had he not told Amy who he'd been with, thanks to Amy's rant, Maggie had gotten a stark reminder she was a surrogate, someone to fill the void left by Virginia Carter. Did he imagine he was with Virginia *every time* he and Maggie were together? Reliving the past in the tall grass by the creek?

Let's go public so the whole world can see how I've made you my own personal blow-up doll.

Torie had warned Maggie she was more involved than she believed, but Maggie had convinced herself otherwise.

Maggie was wrong, and for that split second, when he'd said he wanted to go public, she'd thought he might actually care for her the way she cared for him. Right until he called her Ginny.

The ratfink bastard.

Good thing she hadn't stopped in the real estate office and pursued permanent residence. With two more months remaining on her rental, she had a place to stay if she needed to, but as a remote employee, there was no reason to reside in Edgarville. She needed distance from this small town. Distance from Thad Benson.

A hand closed around her arm and Maggie gasped.

"Out for another little walk I see," Preston said.

"I am not in the mood for you today. What do you want?" she asked.

"Aww," he said tightening his grip. "Have a fight with Lurch, did you? I can give you what you want."

Maggie swung her tote bag at him. "There's nothing I want from you."

He intercepted her tote and tore it free, throwing it to the ground. "Sloane fired me this morning, thanks to you."

Heart pounding, she met his glare. "I expect you brought that on all by yourself."

He yanked her arm and pulled her close. "I'm going to show you who's in charge here." With one hand, he reached for his belt buckle.

No. This wasn't happening. Thad couldn't have gotten far. "Th-th-th!" Damn! This was not the time to stutter!

"The thing about trees," Preston said with a smirk, "is they muffle the sound. Lurch won't be able to hear you, not to mention that if your blog is correct, he's hung up on a dead girl."

She opened her mouth to scream and Preston smashed his lips to hers. She turned her head and spat. "L-l-let me g-g-go."

He laughed at her. "That's better."

He reached for the hem of her sundress and she took the opportunity to knee him in the groin. As he bent over, he grabbed her ankles and she crashed to the ground. Her head connected with a tree trunk and she saw stars.

"Bitch," he growled. He swung wildly and, damn his luck, connected with her jaw.

When no words would come, Maggie screamed.

"Shut up," he told her, his voice strained.

He straddled her on the ground, took her wrists and yanked her arms over her head. Maggie wrestled one hand free and shoved her palm against his nose.

The resultant crunch made her cringe. Blood sprayed her, and when Preston reached for his nose, she rolled out from under him, pushed to her feet, and ran.

"You okay?" a man called from the bike path. A voice she didn't recognize, but she'd take help in whatever form she could. "C-c-call the police," she said, running for her car.

Preston had recovered enough to chase. "I'll kill you, bitch."

The man on the bike pulled a cell phone from his pocket, took a picture and made a call.

Maggie reached the parking lot. She reached for the door handle and prayed the car fob in her tote was close enough to activate the locks. She pushed the button and the locks clicked. She yanked the car open, but before she could get inside, Preston was there, slamming the door against her trailing leg. His fist, covered in blood, came at her once more, connecting with the side of her head.

She closed her eyes against a world that pulsed in and out of focus.

A disembodied voice told Preston to back off. She glimpsed a bike on the ground. Preston face down in the gravel with a knee in his back.

A paramedic hovered over her.

"Can you tell me your name?" the paramedic asked.

"M-m-m-m…" She sighed, tears streaming.

The woman squeezed her hand. "We're taking you to the hospital. You can tell me when you're ready."

Maggie nodded. She pointed to where Preston had thrown her tote bag. A second paramedic pulled her computer out, labeled with her name.

"Maggie Grant?" the second paramedic asked.

She nodded again and explosions of pain went off in her head.

"We'll take care of you, Maggie."

"P-p-p-p…" she said, tears of frustration continuing to fall. She looked for signs of Preston. He sat in the back of the police car, his shirt covered in blood.

"Is there someone we can call for you?" the paramedic asked.

Maggie pointed to her phone. "S-s-s-s-sis…"

"Your sister?" the first paramedic asked.

Maggie nodded, more slowly this time.

She handed the phone to Maggie. Maggie tried to concentrate on the unlock code and couldn't get it on the first try. After two more attempts, she managed a quick text to Torie. "Help."

Torie responded almost immediately. "Are you okay?"

No. Everything hurt and her vision was cloudy. She handed the phone to the paramedic.

"You want me to text her for you?" she asked.

Maggie nodded.

The paramedic turned the phone to show Maggie what she'd sent. "We're taking her to the hospital."

Maggie nodded again and closed her eyes.

Chapter 24

Steady beeping summoned Maggie from the edge of consciousness. An alarm? Someone needed to turn that thing off. Maggie squeezed her eyes more tightly closed.

Images flashed white hot against the dullness in her head. The ambulance. The emergency room. Lying inside a big donut—the CT scan. Torie beside her bed. An orderly wheeling Maggie to a room. A nurse giving her something to help her sleep.

Lots of gaps.

Someone was holding her hand. Thad?

Maggie sneaked a peek and her father leaned over her bed, wrapping his other hand around their joined hands.

"There she is," he said.

A sob came from the corner of the room. Probably her mother.

"Hi, Daddy," Maggie croaked.

"How are you feeling today?" he asked.

She drew a deep breath to test. Dull—everything from her thought processes to the muted lighting in the room to the throbbing in her leg. "I'm not sure," she said. "I suspect I'm heavily medicated."

The shadow moved from the window to stand on the other side of her bed. "How much do you remember?" her mother asked.

Maggie cringed. Amy giving Thad hell for screwing someone in the grass by the creek. Ginny. Preston popping out at her on the trail. The sound of his nose breaking. The pain when he'd slammed the car door on Maggie's leg. "More than I want to," she replied.

Her mother handed her a cup with a bent straw. "Drink?"

Maggie accepted the cup and sipped. Cool water washed down her throat. "Thank you." She handed the cup to her mother and turned to her father once more. "I seem to remember them saying I have a concussion."

"That's right. They wanted to keep you overnight for observation," he said.

"Other than that?" she asked, clearing her throat.

"Contusions, but no breaks."

A nurse breezed into the room. "Good morning! Mom and Dad, can you give us a moment?"

Her mother leaned over the bed and placed a kiss on Maggie's cheek. Her father squeezed Maggie's hand and they left the room.

The nurse wrapped a cuff around Maggie's arm. "How are you feeling this morning?"

"Hung over," Maggie said. "Without benefit of alcohol."

The nurse smiled. "That sounds about right." She took the blood pressure reading and then held the temperature scanner to Maggie's forehead. "The doctor will stop in to see you this morning. You're scheduled with physical therapy to check your mobility, and the social worker will be by to chat with you."

Maggie nodded, and then winced from the effort. "Feels like my brains want to fall out."

"More like they don't have room to move," the nurse said. "Let's get you out of bed and to the bathroom."

Maggie rose to her feet, stiff and sore. The nurse set a walker in front of her.

"Your injuries are enough to warrant vacation time. Go lay on the beach for a few weeks," the nurse told her.

"Fine by me. I'll pack my e-reader and be off," Maggie joked.

"You probably won't feel like reading," the nurse said. "At least not for prolonged periods of time."

"How am I supposed to do my job, then?"

"The doctor will discuss all that with you."

By the time she was back in her bed, the doctor walked in. He greeted the nurse, washed his hands, and smiled at Maggie. "I'm Doctor Morris. Can you tell me your name?"

"Maggie Grant."

He took a penlight from his pocket and shined it in her eyes. "And your date of birth?" he asked.

She recited it for him. "Can my parents come back in?"

"I'll get them for you," The nurse said on her way out.

He pulled back her sheet and examined her leg. "Does this hurt?"

"I'd say yes, and probably worse than I know considering everything feels a little muted this morning."

He pressed two fingers to her foot, first to the top and then on the side, then bent her ankles toward her legs. "Does this hurt?"

"Yes."

Her parents hovered near the door while the doctor measured her calf.

"You have a severe contusion to your leg," The doctor said. "We'll want to keep an eye on that and I want to see you in my office in a couple of days—sooner if your pain increases. I'm going to send you home with crutches, but you should walk as much as you're comfortable doing. Your injuries put you at risk for a deep vein thrombosis. You'll have to go slowly because of your concussion."

He covered her legs again, picked up a chart from the end of the bed and made notes. "Rest is the best thing for you right now. You'll have difficulty watching television, or reading, or using a computer for a few days. Take it slow. If you get a headache, stop."

He set the chart down. "I want you to see the physical therapist before I'll sign your release, and you should continue therapy three times a week for four weeks after you go home. Do you have someone who can help you?"

"I can stay with her," Maggie's mother said. "How long will she need help?"

He did a half turn to acknowledge her. "At least for the first week. She shouldn't drive for at least seven to ten days, but it will be several weeks before she'll be back to normal."

"You don't have to stay, Mom," Maggie said.

"Don't be ridiculous," her mother said. "We'll stay at Torie's. That way she can help, too. I'll have Lacey come here for Fourth of July instead of home to Indiana."

Maggie had wanted to get out of Edgarville. Here was her ticket, although she hadn't expected to move back in with Torie.

One step at a time

"Any questions for me?" the doctor asked.

Maggie shook her head and winced again. "I'm sure I'll have more later."

"Write them all down, and schedule a follow-up at my office," he said. "As long as everything checks out, we'll let you go home this afternoon." He smiled. "You're doing great, Maggie. Keep it up."

As he left, an orderly came in with a wheelchair. "Ready for physical therapy?" he asked.

"Do I have a choice?" Maggie replied.

"We'll come back later to take you home," Maggie's father told her. "We can stop by your rental here in town to pick up a few things if you like and then we'll all head to Foxfield."

"Sounds like a plan," Maggie said, easing into the wheelchair.

Her father held her hand one more time. "You're going to be okay."

She smiled at him. "Aren't I always?"

Her mother sniffled again and the orderly wheeled her away.

Sunlight shone through the windows like lightning bolts to her eyes as they crossed a bridge from the patient rooms to the physical therapy center.

179

A woman in scrubs with spiky hair met them. The orderly handed the woman a chart from the back of the wheelchair and excused himself.

"Good morning!" the woman said, altogether too perky. She turned her badge so Maggie could read it. "I'm Emma McCormick, and I'm a physical trainer. We're going to teach you how to use crutches and then go over the exercises you should do to regain the strength in your leg."

Not another McCormick. Small-town demographics. "Are you related to Amy?" Maggie asked.

"Yes, I am. She's married to my brother-in-law. How do you know Amy?"

"Met her around town." Maggie winced, a wave of nausea washing over her. "How many people know I'm here?"

"I couldn't say. Do you want me to call Amy?" Emma asked.

"No." Maggie said sharply.

Emma folded her arms. "We're bound by HIPAA laws. If you don't want anyone to know you're here, they won't find out, but you will need help during your recovery."

"I have my parents and my sister," Maggie told her. "I'd rather the population at large doesn't know about what happened."

"Gotcha. I will tell you they ran a story in the paper this morning. The police haven't released a lot of details, but people are aware there was an assault on the bike path. The story only says it was a targeted assault and they're holding a person of interest." Emma crouched beside the wheelchair. "You will press charges, won't you?"

"Yes."

"Then people are bound to find out. If you're interested, I teach self-defense classes at the Y."

Maggie smiled. "Been there, done that. Pretty sure I broke his nose. Didn't stop him, but slowed him down enough for me to get help."

Emma held up a palm to high-five her. "Then let's get you back on your feet."

Chapter 25

T had stopped at the café for his morning coffee and looked around—just to be sure. Maggie wasn't there.

She wasn't answering her cell phone. He'd been by the creek. He'd been to the café every day for breakfast *and* lunch. She'd simply disappeared.

Her laughter when he'd told her he wanted to go public continued to haunt him. Whether he was forty-two or twenty, a woman avoiding him cut just as deep—deeper when it was a woman he'd come to care so much about.

When he reached the counter, Sandra handed him his coffee without bothering to ask what he wanted.

"Maggie still sitting for you?" she asked. "She hasn't been into the café for a few days. Wondering if she's okay."

Trolling for gossip. "Haven't seen her." Thad hiked a shoulder. "I figure she got bored. Sitting still for hours at a time isn't a lot of fun."

"Yeah, but she probably sits still while she's reading—which is her job—and isn't your statue a woman reading? So you'd kind of think it didn't matter where she was sitting."

He didn't need everyone pitying him in case they did think he and Maggie had become an item. Which they wouldn't.

He raised his coffee cup and headed for the door. Amy arrived before he could leave.

"Who's in the showroom?" he asked her.

"Brian. Is there a reason I shouldn't come for a cup of apple cider?" she groused.

Oh, yeah. Pregnancy hormones, times two. "Just askin'," he said.

"And what did you do to Maggie? I haven't seen her all week," Amy went on.

He cocked an eyebrow. "Do?"

She poked his chest. "She was the girl in the grass, wasn't she? Did you make a pass at her? Make her uncomfortable? Is that why she's hiding out?"

Thad flinched. He'd more than made a pass at Maggie, and she hadn't seemed at all uncomfortable. Not until he'd suggested going public. No, he wasn't about to tell his little sister about his love life, or lack thereof. The last thing he needed right now was more insults about his ability to attract and keep a woman. *This* was why he was a confirmed bachelor.

He speared Amy with another look before he walked past her toward the monument shop. He had work to do...

Thanks to Amy, damn it all. He couldn't manage to stay angry with her for more than a few paces.

Brian sat at Amy's desk, his feet crossed at the ankles. He nodded when Thad walked in.

"Three new stencils in Amy's folder from yesterday," Brian said. "You want me to take care of them for you?"

Amazing how solicitous Brian had become now that he had an expiration date. Next week he'd be gone and Thad and Amy would be running the monument shop essentially on their own. As long as Brian was here, he could do the headstones while Thad took on another garden statue.

"I'll help you move the stones into the sandblasting booth when they're ready," Thad said.

Brian rose from the chair and headed to the back. Thad took over Amy's seat.

The *Reading Women* blog was open on Amy's computer. A book review. Thad scrolled to the archive list, to the one from last Sunday, the "he makes me want to be a better woman" one.

She was a better woman, and probably someone else's loving partner.

Thad rubbed his chest and scrolled to the first post in the series. She'd said something about Thad's reading her blog. Was there something in her posts he'd missed?

The tightness in his chest constricted.

...and as he rose to leave, he told the dead girl "I still miss you," touched his fingers to his lips and placed the kiss on the top of the stone.

For a moment Thad forgot to breathe.

That first day he'd seen her in the cemetery, she'd also seen him. She'd been watching him. What the hell else did she publish for the rest of the world to see?

Thad read through all seven of the posts, ending with the one he'd read last Monday, and then he went back to the first in the series.

Ginny got the last laugh after all. Twenty-three years later, she was still making fun of him. Who could love a freak of nature like him?

He was a pitiful figure. The only thing missing from the series was Maggie telling him his face had character. It must have been torture for her to look at him when they were together.

He didn't want her pity.

Well, she didn't have to pretend anymore.

Amy walked in, shooting him a heated glance.

He wasn't in the mood.

"I need some air," he said, brushing past her.

"Thad," she called after him.

"No. Not right now."

He kept walking, into the cemetery, to the columbarium walls where he'd first seen Maggie reading, when he'd mistaken her for Amy.

Maggie didn't look anything like Amy.

He glanced across to Ginny's grave. Yep, Maggie had had a ringside seat and she'd made up her own story about him and Ginny.

"Damn it!" he shouted, turning in a circle to make sure he was alone in the cemetery.

He stomped up the hill and stopped in front of Ginny's headstone, the one place he had always felt comfortable talking through things—until he'd met Maggie.

Ginny had been dead twenty-three years. *Twenty-three years.*

"I hope you're pleased with yourself," he muttered. "Still laughing at me, all these years later. I suppose I deserve it, thinking there might be someone out there..." He tilted his head to look at the sky through the trees.

"Next time I'll take Amy's advice and hire a hooker. It's a hell of a lot simpler. Isn't that what you were, at the end of the day?"

Amy's voice floated to him. "You're Haunted Heathcliff, aren't you?"

Beside a tree, she took one step toward him, hesitated, then took a second step.

"What do you want?" he asked, his eyes burning.

Amy looked at the headstone, took another tentative step forward and reached a hand for the granite. Oh, no. She was not going to try to make contact with Ginny Carter, to find out what unfinished thoughts Ginny might have left behind. Thad intercepted Amy's hand.

"What would she tell me?" Amy asked.

"You said she didn't have anything left to say. She isn't one of the voices you hear in the cemetery."

"That's right," Amy said. "So I guess *you'd* better tell me."

He shook his head and a tear dislodged itself from the corner of his eye.

"You and Ginny?" she asked. "Were you in love with her?"

"No."

"What she wrote—Maggie…"

He turned away and started toward the road, but Amy grabbed his arm. "All my life, the three of you have been hovering over me. Protecting me. Not letting anyone get close to me. I loved you for it, for looking out for me, but you always knew so much more about me than I ever knew about you." Tears streamed down her face and she hiccupped with sobs.

Thad rolled his eyes. He hated seeing her cry, even if the tears were brought on by an excess of hormones.

"When she asked about Ginny in the café that first day, when she mentioned she'd seen someone by the stone, her description sounded like one of you, but I told her it couldn't possibly be."

He tried to leave again and she yanked him back.

"Is that why you've been so prickly lately?" she asked. "Don't think I haven't noticed. You've never been upset when I called you a caveman before. You're in love with her, aren't you? With Maggie?"

"And what good would it be if I was?" he said, his voice rough. "Who could love a face like this?" The pain in his chest burned hot.

"Maggie could."

He yanked free and folded his arms. "Apparently not."

"After you left the café, Sandra took a break. She and I went over to the Cascade Building to look for Maggie. I wanted to apologize to her if you'd offended her. Did you know she's taken a leave of absence?"

"No."

"What happened, Thad?"

"None of your business, Amy."

She stepped into his personal space, looking up at him. "That isn't going to work. I'm your sister, and after all the years of torture you put me through, it's my turn to worry about you. I should be apologizing to you for assuming you did something to offend Maggie. If she'd been offended, she would have been asking for help when I found the two of you rolling around in the grass. Why didn't you tell me you were with Maggie?"

He rounded on Amy, fists clenched at his sides. "First of all, we weren't rolling around. We were sitting. I wanted to protect her from gossip. Word gets around town pretty quickly. If she wanted to be with me, it had to be her decision, which is what we were discussing when you interrupted us." He swiped at his eyes. "Doesn't matter. She laughed when I suggested we go public. Now my own sister is feeling sorry for me and you know what? I don't like it. This is why I don't share the intimate details of my personal life."

"You need to have someone you can talk to," she said softly.

He waved at Ginny's headstone. "I did. Someone who didn't talk back to me. Someone who wouldn't judge me."

"Someone who never loved you. A dead person doesn't count." She uncurled one of his fists and laced her fingers with his. "You can talk to me. I won't tell anyone else and I won't judge you." Tears continued to roll down her cheeks. "I can't stand to see you hurting, Thad, and I can't help but feel I'm partly responsible. You're a good man. You deserve to find a woman who will love you, and looking back on the past two weeks," she sniffed, "I have to wonder if I didn't screw this one up."

Thad laughed. "It isn't all about you, Amy."

"No, but I interrupted a very important conversation, and now Maggie's disappeared."

Thad pulled Amy into a hug. "She made a choice. I have to honor that."

Amy squeezed him tight, and he let her.

"Or something's wrong," Amy said. "Was she ill?"

"Not that I know of."

After several minutes, she pushed away, her head bowed. "Can I say something?"

"Can I stop you?"

She slugged him in the shoulder and he made a show of being injured by rubbing it and pouting.

"You've always been a loner. Not letting anyone close. Garth and I always figured you needed your space, but Brian—I think he feels left out sometimes. You should invite him to see your man-cave. Before he leaves. With Maggie disappearing…"

Thad tilted his head. "You don't really think he believes I'm secretly a serial killer and my workshop is my lair, do you?"

"No, but I think you might make the gesture. He feels left out sometimes."

Thad put a hand over his eyes and turned away.

"Are you still working on her statue?"

"Yes."

"Take the mystery out of your man-cave," Amy said again. "He's going through some stuff these days, too. He could use a big brother, one who isn't always giving him a hard time."

Yeah, Thad knew that. He shook his head and snorted. "Fine."

Anything to make Amy stop crying.

Chapter 26

Maggie sat at the patio table outside Torie's townhouse wearing her floppy hat and watching a rabbit nibble at a patch of clover. The patio was one of the only places she felt safe sitting outside, surrounded by flowers and shrubs, within running distance of a door she could lock if she needed it.

Torie opened the sliding glass doors and reached inside for a couple of glasses of lemonade. Small flags stuck out of her pockets. She handed a glass to Maggie and set the second glass on the patio table. She stuck the flags into the ground.

"It's nice and cool inside," she said, closing the screen door behind her.

"Thanks for the drink," Maggie said quietly, not acknowledging Torie's attempt to lure her inside.

"Mom and Dad should be back from the airport with Lacey any time now."

Maggie closed her eyes and tilted her face to the sky.

"Which is why I came out to talk to you. I'm worried about you," Torie said.

Maggie opened one eye and focused on her sister. "Why?"

"You aren't yourself."

"Then who am I?" She opened both eyes and took a drink.

"The Maggie I know doesn't let the world get to her. She's bright and optimistic and outgoing. Since the... the..."

Maggie cracked a smile. "So now you have a stutter?"

Torie huffed. "I don't know how to refer to what happened to you."

"Assault."

Torie reached for Maggie's hands. "You seem so depressed."

"I hurt. Or the concussion dulled my normally bubbly personality."

"You do have a bubbly personality."

Maggie scowled. "Maybe it's the prospect of more people coming to feel sorry for me."

"People who care about you." Torie released Maggie's hands. "Maybe we could all go for a walk when everyone gets here, get you out into the world."

Out into the world. A shiver ran along Maggie's spine. She needed to get out of the house more. So far, she'd only gotten as far as group counseling sessions, which Torie escorted her to and from.

She hated that she was too afraid to go anywhere alone.

Lacey's voice carried through the townhouse. "If she didn't want to go to Indiana, she might have said something sooner. We had to pay extra to change our reservations to fly into Chicago."

"She needs rest," their mother said.

Maggie turned her back on the door. If such a thing as a transporter existed, she'd wish herself in

Edgarville, to her shabby rental, where no one had to fuss over her.

The screen door slid open amidst more chatter and the sounds of creaking lawn chairs.

A hand settled on her armrest, and then her father knelt before her. "Hey, Magpie."

She smiled, tears welling in her eyes. "Hi, Daddy."

"Still too sore for a hug?"

She leaned forward and wrapped her arms around him. Sometimes a girl needed her dad.

"My sisters, Torie and Maggie," Lacey said behind her.

Her father stared into Maggie's eyes, silently asking if she was ready. She nodded, bowed her head and pushed to her feet.

Lacey gasped. So much for hoping they wouldn't notice the fading bruises.

Maggie extended her hand and limped her first couple of steps until her circulation caught up. Lacey's current boyfriend, blond and tanned, was the epitome of a California surfer. "Nice to meet you. I'm afraid I don't know your name." A shadow of pain raced across her temples with the sudden movement.

"Carson," he said, taking her hand. "Sorry to hear about your accident."

Accident. As if Preston's fists had accidentally connected with her head. As if the car door had accidentally slammed into her leg.

And Lacey—her face reflected pure horror.

"Torie said someone had attacked you, but I kind of thought it was…" Lacey said. "You know…"

"Rape?" Maggie supplied. "He didn't get the chance to assault me sexually." She grimaced when Lacey touched one of the bruises on her face.

"Why did he do this to you?" Lacey asked.

Because he had his own set of issues which he'd transferred to Maggie? Her injuries would give Lacey a first-hand look at what happened when you condemned someone for something beyond their control. "Because I stutter," she said clearly.

Lacey took a step back as if she'd been struck. Good.

"Do you?" Carson asked. "Stutter? I haven't noticed."

"Years of therapy," Maggie told him. "It's mostly resolved now." She forced a smile for her mother and gave her a hug. "Morning, Mom."

"Let me get the pitcher of lemonade if you all insist on sitting outside in this heat," Torie said, walking into the townhouse.

"I'll help," Mom said.

"Sorry you had to rearrange your travel plans," Maggie told Lacey.

"I didn't realize how badly you'd been hurt," Lacey said. "Torie said you didn't want anyone to worry, so I assumed it wasn't a big deal." She held both of Maggie's hands. "You should have told me."

Maggie scowled at her. The sympathy had to be a show for Carson's benefit.

"The guy's in jail and I'm on the mend," Maggie replied. She turned her chair to face the rest of them and resumed her seat.

"There's my Suzy Sunshine," Torie said, carrying a tray of glasses while her mother brought the pitcher.

193

"I'm not your anything," Maggie said.

"Torie's been telling us about your new boyfriend," Mom said. "We were hoping to meet him today, too."

Maggie shot Torie a withering look. "He's not exactly a boyfriend. Just someone I met who inspired a week's worth of blog posts. You know me. I cast him in the role of Heathcliff from Wuthering Heights, the continuing saga after Catherine dies."

Her father reached across from the chair beside to rest a hand on Maggie's shoulder and squeezed gently. "One of these days, you're going to have to let the hero stick around."

"Or accept my fate as a spinster sister," Maggie joked, more to ease the ache in her heart than to lighten the mood. "What do you say, Mabel?" she said in a little old lady voice, nodding to Torie.

"I prefer the term independent woman to spinster," Torie said. "Dad, can you start the grill? We've got snacks to eat while we wait."

Lacey leaned closer to Maggie. "The guy that did this to you. Because you had a stutter?" she asked again.

"Yes," Maggie said. "For some people, verbal abuse isn't enough."

Lacey backed away as if she'd been struck. "Passive-aggressive much?"

"Oh, was that a little too close to home?"

"Girls," their mother said. "Can't you get along for one day?"

Maggie glanced at Carson. No, she wasn't going to ask for an apology in front of Lacey's current boyfriend. Let the poor schmuck find out on his own what kind of woman he was involved with, the same way Lacey's ex-husband had. Lacey couldn't seem to help herself where Maggie was concerned. The first time she'd introduced husband number one to Maggie, after the elopement—because Lacey was embarrassed by her whole family—he'd had a ringside seat to Lacey's brand of disdain for a sister who stutters, from "oh, don't pay any attention to her," to "now you know what I've had to deal with all my life," to "That's why I didn't want her at our wedding." Whether Maggie was his first glimpse into Lacey's warped personality or the catalyst after a long line of incidents, Lacey had placed the blame for her abandonment squarely on Maggie's shoulders.

Maggie prepared herself for the next barb, but Lacey surprised her.

"I'm sorry."

Maggie blinked several times, not sure she'd heard correctly. She glanced around. Who was Lacey apologizing to? Their mother?

Lacey bowed her head. "Can we take a walk?"

Maggie glanced around again.

"Sure," Carson said.

"No," Lacey said. She took one of his hands and smiled at him. "I meant Maggie." She looked at Maggie then. "Can you walk?"

"Part of my physical therapy," Maggie said. She stared at Lacey a moment before she nodded.

"We can all go," Torie said.

"I was hoping for a few minutes alone with Maggie," Lacey said.

"You going to be okay?" Torie asked Maggie.

"I think we can manage," Maggie said. "If we're not back in fifteen minutes, send a wheelchair." She eased to her feet and grabbed her cane. She hadn't needed it for several days, but better to have it in case she lost her balance.

Her heart pounded as she led Lacey along the path of stepping stones around the side of the townhouse to the sidewalk out front.

Strength in numbers. She wasn't alone. But did she trust Lacey?

"He attacked you because you stutter?" Lacey asked again as they walked past the neighbor's house.

"I think I've already said that." Maggie took a deep breath and stopped walking. "If you intend to prove that somehow I provoked this attack…"

Lacey took Maggie's arms. "No. That's not what I meant." Her lips trembled. "I was horrible to you. I know that now, but I want you to understand why. People referred to me as the sister of that girl who stutters, as if somehow I carried an infection. I felt isolated. Ostracized. They judged me, and the only way I could separate myself from you was to make fun of you with them. It was the wrong thing to do."

"Ya think?"

"When you guys met Brock, I was worried he'd judge me by you once again," Lacey went on. "He did, but not the way I thought he might. I had to take a long, hard look at myself when he left me, and it wasn't pretty. For years, I told myself it was the Maggie effect. By the time I figured out it was the Lacey effect, I didn't know how to make things better." Her voice cracked. "And you and Torie have always been so close, I felt even more isolated."

"You never wanted to hang out," Maggie said. "Avoided me like the plague. As for Torie, you have a relationship with her. Maybe because the both of you suffered from the Maggie effect."

Lacey hung her head. "No. She never did. And that only made things worse."

"So what you're saying is you treated me like the plague as a result of the friends you made. Choices you made."

Lacey nodded. "Bad choices. I'm sorry, Maggie. I know this is a lifetime coming, but seeing you like this, all bruised and broken... I never wanted to see you hurt."

Maggie stared at her. She'd never considered how her disorder might reflect on her sisters. "You might have said something when we were kids," she said. "When those mean girl friends of yours made you feel bad."

"Young and stupid. Isn't that always the excuse? I guess it took me longer than some to grow up and stop looking for affirmation from the wrong people." She drew a deep breath. "I'm sorry."

Maggie's leg ached and her head throbbed from unshed tears. She could only nod. Torie's house—her sanctuary while she recovered—was still in view. "Do you mind if we go back? I don't think I can make it around the block."

With the Citronella torches lit, the family sat on the patio watching fireworks light the sky. Like he had when they were kids, Maggie's father quietly sang what he called "songs of the soil"—songs his parents had sung to him when he was a child. They all joined in, having heard the songs hundreds of times over the years.

For the first time in the last two weeks, Maggie felt whole, the little girl in the safe harbor that was her family. Even Lacey seemed more at peace.

Maggie excused herself to use the bathroom, and when she was finished, Torie met her in the hall. "Your turn?" she asked.

Torie slid an arm around Maggie's waist. "Everything okay with you and Lacey?"

"I'm not the sort to hold a grudge," she said. Hearing how her speech disorder had colored Lacey's life did make a difference. She expected better from her sister. Torie hadn't treated Maggie like a pariah.

"What happened to your Haunted Heathcliff? You haven't said anything about him since the attack, and I've been tiptoeing around the subject. Since Mom brought him up…"

Maggie shrugged.

"Have you talked to him since the attack?"

"No. I'm not sure he knows about it."

Torie took a step back. "It's a small town. How can he not know?"

"HIPAA laws."

"Huh?"

"The paramedics couldn't say anything, or the doctors. I don't think anyone knows. I don't want anyone to know."

"What about your new friends? You were going to invite them to book club. What did you tell them?"

Maggie stared at her hands. "I haven't turned my phone on since the assault."

Torie rolled her eyes. "Dorothy has left the building," she said. "They melted the wicked witch, you know. What if someone wants to visit you in Kansas?"

Maggie scowled. "Amy sent an email to my work address. I've been trying to decide how to answer it. She sent me a photo of the statue."

"It would be rude not to answer," Torie said. "Right?"

Maggie chuckled. "She also said she'd figured out who my Haunted Heathcliff was and she apologized for interrupting a 'very important conversation.' I guess I'm glad she did, and maybe that's what I'll tell her. She gave him the chance to go public right then and there, and he didn't."

"So that's the reason you're giving him the cold shoulder. The same cold shoulder you've been giving everyone."

Maggie cringed. "I need more time to heal."

"You're making excuses, Maggie. You've never done that before."

"No, I'm recovering," Maggie argued. "I don't need more people making a fuss over me."

"Sometimes people need to make a fuss over those they care about. You need to let them."

"What are you two talking about?" Lacey asked, joining them in the hallway.

Thank heavens for distractions. "So, you and Carson," Maggie said, switching gears. "New husband material?"

"I'm taking it slow this time," she said. "Some lessons are harder to learn than others, especially when confronted with your own character flaws."

199

Shades of Sandra and Amy in the café flooded back. Hadn't Sandra said something about being a mean girl once? And Amy had forgiven her. The two were as close as sisters now.

Maggie hugged Lacey. "Nothing but love for you, sister."

Chapter 27

While Brian smoothed the epoxy around the base of the stone, Thad pulled off his gloves. For a moment in time, with all three of them in the cemetery setting a monument, Thad could forget how alone he felt running the business.

"That oughtta do it," Brian said, standing.

Which meant he'd likely be heading back to Widdersfield. Thad had yet to follow through on Amy's suggestion to invite him to see the workshop. "Hey, if you're not in a hurry to go, thought you might like to come over and see the statue I finished," he said.

Brian pulled off his gloves and set his hands on his hips. "You're actually inviting me to your man-cave?"

Thad shrugged. "Thought you might like to see for yourself that it isn't a dungeon and I'm not holding anyone against their will."

"That was a joke, in case you didn't know," Brian said. "No one thinks you beat up Maggie."

"Not funny," Thad said.

"Wasn't meant to be."

Thad's pulse ratcheted up. "So why say it?"

Brian studied him a minute. "You don't know?"

"Don't know what?"

"I saw her in Foxfield. I've been seeing that friend of hers off and on, you know, and I caught a glimpse of

Maggie there." He cocked his head. "When's the last time you talked to her? Maggie?"

Thad turned his palms up and curled his fingers, inviting answers. "What don't I know?"

"You remember that news story about the guy on the bike path?"

"You're going to have to give me more than that."

Brian huffed. "Some guy beat Maggie up on the bike path."

Some guy?

Thad's pulse kicked into overdrive.

Brian turned to Garth. "You heard about it, right?"

Garth knew, too?

"And you're just telling me now?" Thad asked.

Brian glanced at Garth, then back at Thad. "Thought you knew."

He had to find out what happened, and he couldn't do that hanging around the cemetery. "Are we done here?"

Garth shouldered into Brian, nudging him toward the road.

Thad stomped toward the truck and climbed behind the wheel.

Garth slid into the middle, Brian beside him. "It's too hot," Garth said. "Let's head to Murphy's. I'll buy."

"I'm meeting Jean for a drink," Brian said. "She's meeting me when she gets off work."

"Then you have time to lift one with your brothers," Garth said.

Beat up?

Thad started the truck and headed to the monument shop. "I'll sit this one out."

"Like hell," Garth said. "Unless you want to string one of us up in your workshop. I could help you tie Brian's wrists together if you want to hang him from the rafters."

"Ha-ha," Thad said.

"C'mon. You owe me a beer," Brian said. "Then I'll be on my way with Jean and you can go to your cave and hide."

He didn't want to go to his cave. He wanted to drive to Foxfield and find out what happened to Maggie. Except he didn't know where Maggie's sister lived. "Fine," he said.

They were at the shop within moments. "Can you lock up?" Thad asked Amy as they walked through the showroom.

"Yes sir, boss," she replied.

Thad and his brothers headed toward Main Street, three abreast. Just like old times, but not the same.

"Beat up?" he asked Brian once more.

"I thought you knew something the rest of us didn't," Brian replied. "You aren't always a wellspring of information, you know."

"Are you sure we're talking about Maggie?"

"Black eye, bruised cheek, and she was limping. I don't think she saw me, though."

"How long ago did you see her?" Thad asked.

"I don't know, it was before the Fourth of July, but after I moved to Widdersfield. A week ago?"

Was that why she'd disappeared?

How could he not know what happened?

They walked into Murphy's and Thad scanned the bar. Russ Weber was there, out of uniform. He'd know what happened to Maggie, wouldn't he?

203

"You guys grab a table," Thad said. "I want to ask Russ something quick." He approached the policeman and rested a hand on his shoulder.

"Hey, Thad," Russ said.

"Listen, I got a question. You remember Maggie Grant? The woman from the magazine? She was only around a couple of weeks, but someone mentioned she'd had some sort of accident. You know anything about a police report?"

"Yeah, I remember her. Got beat up pretty bad. They took her to the hospital."

Thad's heart came to a dead stop. "Beat up?"

"Turns out the assailant was an asshole she worked with. He got laid off and decided it was her fault, apparently. He's cooling his heels in the county jail."

The bully who'd made fun of her? "Any idea where she went?"

"Pretty sure she went to live with her sister while she was recovering. Why?" He nudged Thad. "Thinking of asking her out?" He sat back and assessed Thad. "Wait a minute. You did ask her out. Didn't you take her to dinner when she first came to town?"

He was not going to get into this discussion. Thad managed a smile. "Wondered what happened to her, that's all."

When he took his seat at his brothers' table, Delia arrived with their beers. Wonder of wonders, Brian didn't even bother looking at her, much less say thank you.

"Thank you, Delia," Thad said.

She smiled. "You bet."

"This next six months is gonna be the longest six months in history," Garth said, toasting Brian.

"Why?" Thad asked.

"Amy. She cries if you look at her sideways. Even Sandra is afraid to talk to her." He toasted Thad's mug and took a swallow.

"You're falling behind," Brian said. "Shouldn't you and Sandra be providing more cousins to that brood?"

"Got our hands full with the one," Garth replied, and then he smiled a dreamy sort of smile. "Best thing I ever did." He checked his watch and drained his glass. "Speaking of which, I should be getting home." He rose from the table and reached across to shake Brian's hand. "Good to see you. Don't be a stranger or your nephew will forget who you are."

"I'm around often enough," Brian said.

Garth squeezed Thad's shoulder. "You okay?"

Far from it. "Why wouldn't I be?" Thad asked.

"Call me if you need me," Garth said on his way out.

"You'd really let me see your man-cave?" Brian asked Thad.

"Nothing much to see, but yeah." He shrugged. "You are a man, after all."

Brian chuckled. "Then I'd have to tell the police where you buried the bodies."

"No bodies, just monuments."

A woman approached the table. "Getting a head start?"

"Brother bonding time," Brian said. "You've met Thad?"

She stepped back and looked him over. "I don't think I have, at least not in person." She extended a hand. "Jean."

Thad rose to his feet and shook her hand. "You're Maggie's friend?" He nodded toward Russ Weber at the bar. "I only just heard what happened to her. That happen at the office?"

She raised her eyebrows. "No."

Why was she looking at Thad like he'd beat her up instead of the bully?

"So what's the story with the dead girl?" she asked.

She knew. Thad glanced around the bar. How many other people knew he was the subject of Maggie's blog posts?

"I don't follow," he said.

"First you call her by that dead girl's name, then she hears your sister having a flashback." Her hands went to her hips. "Funny way to go public, letting her hide down there."

"Wait a minute. What are you talking about?"

"If you'd have introduced her to your sister instead of hiding her in the grass, she might not have run into that jackhole."

Thad pressed his fingers to his temples. "Back up. He beat her up by the creek? That day?"

Brian furrowed his brow. "What's going on?"

Jean cocked her head toward Thad. "Ask your brother."

"Now wait a minute," Thad said. "When I told her I wanted to go public, she laughed at me. She could have shown her face anytime she wanted, but she chose not to."

"Laughed at you?" Jean repeated. "Maggie never laughed at anyone a day in her life. Hello? Have you met this woman? She knows what it's like to be on the receiving end. Have you considered she was laughing because she was happy you wanted to go public? Right before you steered your sister away from your secret rendezvous."

"Rendezvous?" Brian repeated.

Thad took a deep breath. "Where is she? She won't answer the phone."

"She's on medical leave," Jean told him. "What you did to her was pretty shitty. Not as bad as Preston, but I'm sure it hurts just as much. That woman has a heart of gold, and you broke it."

Damn. This was not the place he wanted to talk about this, and not in front of these people, but he had to know. "Yeah, maybe she broke my heart, too."

Brian dropped to his seat. "The man never says a word, and suddenly he's a fountain of information."

"Shut up," Thad barked.

Brian raised a hand. "Shutting."

Jean furrowed her brow. "You telling me you didn't know?"

Thad rolled his eyes. "Until today? Not a word. Not until this numbskull said he'd seen her in Foxfield." He nodded toward the bar again. "I had to ask the cop what happened. I had no idea."

"What dead girl?" Brian asked.

"Shut up, Brian," Thad and Jean said at the same time.

Again, he raised his hand. "Shutting."

"She put my life in a public forum," Thad said.

"No, she created a character from something she'd seen. A little too close for comfort?" Jean asked.

"Not even close."

"Then she didn't put your life in a public forum. She made up a story, and the boss loved it. Told her to run with it. One more thing that pissed off that jackhole. He tried to turn it against Maggie, but he didn't know the boss made her write it."

"What public forum?" Brian asked. "I'm finding out more today than I ever knew about my brother."

Thad ignored him. His flight response was in high gear. "Can you convince her to talk to me?" he asked Jean.

Jean folded her arms and eyed him speculatively. "I don't know what Maggie sees in you."

Thad exhaled a sigh. "We never got the chance to talk. We started, and then Amy showed up..." He rubbed his forehead with his hand. "Not Amy's fault. I should have said something sooner."

Jean dropped her arms, eyeing him warily. "She'll have to clean out the place she was renting. I think she's planning to move in with her sister again, but I couldn't say for sure. She's been pretty quiet these last few weeks." She heaved a sigh. "I can let you know when she'll be here."

"I'd appreciate it." Thad glanced at Brian, who sat with his arms folded, watching the exchange.

"What dead girl?" Brian asked again.

"Doesn't matter," Thad said. "Part of the past."

Chapter 28

A nother week had passed, and still Maggie didn't know how to respond to Amy. Or if she should. Of course she should.

Sitting under the umbrella on Torie's patio, she stared at the flashing cursor in her blank reply. Maggie couldn't use the 'my head hurts when I read' excuse anymore. On the outside, her bruises had faded from black and purple to an ugly shade of yellow. Instead of looking battered, she looked jaundiced.

On the inside...

On the inside she'd taken a different sort of beating. Thanks to Preston, she was afraid to go out alone, but the deeper pain was the hole in her heart left by Edgarville's confirmed bachelor.

She had friends there. Walking alone on Main Street wouldn't be a problem, and she could avoid being alone in the more remote areas. She was more afraid of running into Thad. He might have said he wanted to go public, but as a confirmed bachelor, he'd never be able to give her what she wanted—and she wanted more than to be his blow-up doll.

Like the bruises, she would heal. Life would go on, but for now, she couldn't bring herself to go back to Edgarville.

Of all the people in Edgarville, Amy had been the one to reach out to her. Maggie needed to acknowledge that, despite Amy's backward apologies.

She opened the picture Amy had sent and read through the email one more time.

I thought you should see the finished product, she wrote. *Thad let me into his studio to see his work, and I have to admit I was a little creeped out by the faces looking back at me. I hope you'll forgive him his obsession, and I hope he didn't frighten you. I know he's not the most handsome man in the world, but I believe he cares about you—especially once I saw the statue.*

We've missed seeing you around town, and I hope Thad didn't offend you or embarrass you in some way.

Sandra asked me to say hello, and she has a cup of blueberry tea waiting for you next time you stop in.

All the best – Amy McCormick

Amy continued to make excuses for a man who didn't need any. No, Thad might not be the most attractive man in the world, but he was a far cry from ugly, and a good soul was far more attractive than a handsome face.

He was a "real man," more than any man she'd ever met, and the 'creepy faces' in his studio demonstrated how deep the well of his soul was.

The picture Amy had sent was remarkable. Thad was a gifted artist, and a certain amount of vanity made her want to see the statue he'd done of her up close.

Amy, she typed.

I apologize for the delay in responding. I've had some difficulties reading these last few weeks and am only now returning to a more normal state.

210

Thank you so much for sending the picture. Thad certainly is a talented artist, and I'm humbled that he chose me as a model.

As to the creepy faces, I'm sure each of those ladies meant something to him, and those carvings were his way to remember them.

I'm on a leave of absence from the magazine, but I'll be sure to stop by and see Sandra next time I'm in town.

Maggie hit send and sat back to stare at the picture once more.

I'm sure each of those ladies meant something to him.

Did Maggie mean something to him?

He meant something to her.

She was determined to return to Edgarville, if only to show everyone in town there was more to Thad than they gave him credit for. She was becoming increasingly restless sitting around this townhouse all day, every day.

She contemplated the drive to Edgarville. Tomorrow.

If she could talk herself into leaving the townhouse.

She could ride to the office with Jean tomorrow, spend the day at the rental in Edgarville, and then ride home with Jean tomorrow night.

If she could talk herself into being alone at the rental.

Maggie eased away from the patio table and walked into the townhouse. She couldn't be afraid forever. Preston Andrews was safely behind bars.

She would not let that jackhole dictate the rest of her life.

Maggie opened the front door, checked her pocket for her keys and her cell phone—time to turn the beast on—and took a step outside, into the real world. Her heart hammered. The neighbor across the street waved to her and called a greeting. Maggie raised her hand to wave back, trembling, and nearly retreated.

She took a deep breath and took another step outside. She could do this.

Another neighbor was out walking her dog. "Maggie, good to see you," she called out.

Friendly people. No one was going to hurt her.

Except Maggie wasn't ready.

She turned and went into the townhouse. She'd talk about it in her group counseling session tonight.

Chapter 29

"I got an email from Maggie," Amy said as Thad walked into the monument shop.

He stopped before disappearing into the shop, but didn't turn to face her. Maggie had emailed Amy but not him?

"I sent her a picture of the statue," Amy went on. "Thought you'd want to know."

So Maggie hadn't sent an email, she'd replied to one. He nodded and continued.

He had a list of orders to fill.

Since his presentation at the Cemetery Association meeting, business had picked up. The funeral directors who'd been skeptical had agreed to help promote the customized headstones angle, and the addition of the statues on the Benson Monuments web page continued to bring in added revenue.

He could have used Brian's hands, but Brian had his own path to follow. Thad was keeping up so far, but if the pace continued, he'd have to look for help.

With his tablet in hand, he scrolled to check his emails for new orders.

Email.

Maggie had sent Amy an email. Would she answer a phone call? She must have seen the missed calls from him, and she hadn't returned his call. He hadn't tried for more than a week, but if Amy had gotten an email…

Thad took out his phone and dialed her number—and didn't know what to say when she actually answered.

He cleared his throat. "Heard you had some trouble," he said.

"I did."

He held his head with his free hand. "It happened that day? By the creek?"

"It did."

How could he have failed to protect the one woman who meant so much to him? "Dammit. I should have told Amy you were there. If I had, you might not have run into that asshole." The guilt crippled him.

He shouldn't have left her alone. He could have protected her.

"Maggie, I'm so sorry. When you laughed, I thought it was because you found the idea of going public ridiculous."

Her voice sounded frail. "No, actually, I didn't."

"And then I read the rest of your blog posts, the ones about me."

"I'm sorry," she whispered. "I wrote that before I knew who you were. I know what a private person you are. I shouldn't have put your grief on display like that."

"It wasn't grief you saw."

"You aren't haunted by the memory of Virginia Carter?"

He snorted. She didn't believe that, did she? "This doesn't feel like something we should talk about over the phone. Will you be coming back to Edgarville?" He glanced at the showroom door, hoping Amy didn't decide to check on him.

"I extended my lease there another month, but I haven't been... I couldn't..." He heard her sigh. "I'm still recovering. Mentally more than physically."

"I could come there," he offered.

"No."

His heart dropped in his chest. When she'd answered, he had hoped Maggie's friend was right, that Maggie could love a troglodyte like him, even with forty-two years of experience warning him otherwise.

"I have to be able to face things on my own," Maggie went on.

A spark of hope flared again.

"Then let me tell you about Ginny Carter," he said, eyes glued to the showroom door. "And if I don't finish—I'm at the monument shop and I don't want to share this with the world—I'll call you tonight. If that's okay."

"You don't owe me an explanation," she said.

"But I want you to know. Ginny Carter was my first sexual experience. Sandra said she overheard Pru and Rachel telling you about her, so I think you got a good picture of the type of person Ginny was. The thing about Ginny—she didn't judge me. Didn't care what I looked like or what other people thought about me." He chuckled. "Check that. She cared enough that she didn't want to be seen in public with me. It was the first time a woman was willing to get that close to me. No, I didn't love her, but I did wonder if she was the best I could do. When she died..." He rubbed his forehead again.

Now that he'd started, he couldn't seem to stop. "I met a nurse at the hospital who told me what a good heart I had for visiting Ginny when she was in a coma, and I thought I'd made progress on the relationship front. We dated for a short while, until she threw me over, too. I sort of connected her to Ginny, as if Ginny might have brought us together. I stopped by Ginny's grave to thank her. I guess that became a habit, talking to Ginny after she died.

"Ginny had a tough life. She never got the chance to be the person she wanted to be, and she was never able to overcome the reputation she'd garnered here in Edgarville. Yes, I cared for her, in my own way, but no, I don't pine for my lost lover. However, I do miss my friend."

"That's more than I've ever heard you say at one time," Maggie said. "As a romantic, you touched my heart with your devotion, whether she was your lover or your friend. I'm sorry if I embarrassed you, but the odd part was no one seemed to recognize you from the blog. No one knew who the mystery man in the cemetery was."

"Amy figured it out. After you left."

"Then maybe she'll realize you have feelings and stop treating you like a doorpost."

He laughed. "Believe me, she's overcompensating now."

Maggie was silent for a long moment. "I'm sorry if you thought I was making fun of you."

"I should have known better. Your friend pointed that out to me, too."

Maggie chuckled. "I'll have to have a talk with my friend."

"Thank her. I wouldn't have known what happened to you if she hadn't told me. I wish you would have told me."

"I've had a hard time…" She drew another deep sigh. "I went out this morning. By myself. Walked around the block. First time since…"

The desire to kill the asshole bully raged through Thad. "I hate that he did that to you. I should have been there to protect you. Maggie, I meant what I said. I want to go public. I want people to know we're a couple."

"Are we?"

Another thud in his chest. Why would things be different this time? He wanted to tell her he loved her, wanted to plead with her to give him a chance, but he'd learned his lesson long ago. He swallowed the lump in his throat. "I guess that's up to you."

Amy, always with the perfect timing, chose that moment to walk through the showroom door.

"Gotta go," he said, and disconnected.

The ball was in Maggie's court.

~ ~ ~

Thad set a beer and plate of pasta on the coffee table and collapsed onto his sofa. He rested his neck against the back and closed his eyes. Another long day at the shop, for which he was grateful. Benson Monuments truly was a family business, and he was grateful to Amy and Garth for pushing him to expand, but he was dog-tired.

His phone roused him, reminding him how tired he was. The head on his beer was gone and his pasta had grown cold.

"Yeah," he answered without checking the display.

"I have one question," Maggie said.

He leaned over his knees, wide awake. "Shoot."

"In your workshop, behind the house. Three faces, all different renderings."

Ginny, Helena and Danae. "Yeah."

"And me."

"And you," he confirmed.

"Certainly you've had other girlfriends. At least I'm assuming they were all girlfriends."

"I did Ginny to remember her," he said. "She had a good soul, even if it was a lost soul. Same for the others, the good soul part. Each of them saw past the beast to the man inside. Including you. At least for a little while."

"You're not a beast."

He smirked. Part of that good soul thing. He wouldn't have expected anything less from her. "That's your only question?"

She hesitated. "I do have one more, since you're being so amenable."

He laughed. "Hit me with your best shot."

"What makes you a confirmed bachelor?"

The spark of hope lit in his chest again. "Self-preservation as much as anything else, although I'm considering giving up the confirmed part."

Her voice took on the sultry tone that wrapped around him. "Because of me?" she asked.

"Yes." No point in denying it. He wanted Maggie in his life, and the only way to get her there was to take a chance. One more time.

"I'm coming to Edgarville t-t-tomorrow." The first stutter he'd heard from her today. A good bet she was nervous. "B-b-by myself," she added.

"Sounds like a big step."

When she didn't respond, he pictured her nodding.

"I won't let anyone hurt you," he said.

"I n-n-need to do this by myself."

Amy had always told him how much she hated having her brothers hovering over her. Without them, she'd grown into a strong woman. Maggie already was a strong woman, but she needed to regain that strength. As much as he wanted to protect her, he recognized her need to reassure herself. "Then I'll hope to see you tomorrow."

"Good night, Thad," she said softly.

"Good night, Maggie." He stared at his phone, hoping he'd said the right things.

Chapter 30

D riving to Edgarville hadn't been as difficult as Maggie had anticipated. Of course, she was surrounded by three thousand pounds of car. As she parked in front of Benson Monuments, she took a long, slow breath, staring down the car door.

She could do this.

Where once she waited until no one was in sight to move around for fear of running into a bully, now Maggie waited until she saw someone walking the street—someone she could call for help—before she opened the door.

On rubbery legs, she walked into the monument showroom. Could this really be the first time she'd been here? A fountain bubbled happily inside the door. Headstones lined the floor in various shapes and colors of stone. Plaques on the wall were inscribed with different fonts, and in another corner, garden statues.

"Welcome to Benson Monuments. How can I help you?" Amy asked, rolling her chair from behind a partition. She rose to her feet, mouth agape. "Maggie?"

"Hi," Maggie said.

Amy closed the space between them and hugged her.

Maggie laughed. "What did I do to deserve that?"

"It's good to see you. We've missed you."

"Thank you for sending me the picture. I'd wondered if he was able to finish it." She headed for the garden statues and looked them over. "Is he here?" Maggie asked.

Amy cocked her head toward a door in the back of the showroom.

Maggie straightened her shirt, threw her shoulders back and set her course. "I hope he's ready for a break," she said half to herself. Now that she was here, those birds in her chest were flying again. She opened the door.

Garth and Thad were carrying a stone across what looked like a garage full of other stones, away from a booth on the one side. A computer panel was set near the booth. Both men ignored the interruption, muscles bulging with exertion.

"Amy, if you wouldn't mind peeling the stencil off so we can get another stone into the booth," Garth said.

Thad was the first to see her. He straightened and Maggie swore his muscles rippled. Memories of their first night together washed over her, at the picture of him wearing nothing but his gym shorts, glistening with sweat. She shook her head to clear the image. He was dressed in dirty jeans paired with a long-sleeve shirt that hugged tight to his arms and shoulders.

As they set the stone down, Garth raised his head, glanced at Thad, then over to Maggie. "Oh." His gaze went over Maggie's shoulder, where Amy followed behind.

Show time.

Thad had said he wanted to go public, and it was time his family saw him for something other than a silent, shell of a man. Maggie walked up to him, grabbed the front of his shirt to pull him down and kissed him, long and deep. His hands slid around her back and pulled her tight.

"You want to do it right here or go down by the creek?" she whispered when they came up for air.

Amy gasped and Garth chuckled.

The creases in his cheek deepened with his smile, and the lines around his eyes crinkled. Maggie looked at the dent in the tip of his nose, exactly the way she remembered it. Oh, how she'd missed this man, the man who said he was contemplating giving up his 'confirmed' bachelor status. If she had her way, he'd give up the bachelor part, too.

"You really want to do this?" he asked in that deep voice.

"It's time the rest of this town knows you the way I do."

Garth cleared his throat. "He's on the clock right now, ma'am. You're going to have to wait until the end of the day."

Behind her, she heard a sob. "Why is Amy crying?" she asked Thad.

"Overabundance of hormones. She's pregnant."

"Can't a girl be a little emotional without it being hormones every time?" Amy asked and stomped into the showroom.

"Twins," Garth added. "And I'm serious as a heart attack. He needs my help today and I've only got a couple of hours. You can have him all night, if you really want him."

She grinned. "I do, but can I ask one favor while we're here?"

"Anything you want," Thad said.

Maggie looked at Garth. "Five minutes."

Garth nodded.

"Walk with me by the creek? I need to go back to where it happened, and that's something I'm not prepared to do alone." She shot a nervous glance at Garth. "Just a walk there and back."

"Help me put the next stone into the sandblasting booth and I can at least get that started while you're gone," Garth said. "In case it takes more than five minutes."

Thad shot Garth an annoyed glare, but moved to a stone that bore a stencil. He crouched to take one side of the stone while Garth took the other.

Welcome to the gun show. No wonder these guys were so buff. They carried the stone into the booth.

"I've got it from here," Garth said, his voice muted.

Thad walked out and took Maggie's hand. "You sure you want to do this?"

She smiled. "No more ghosts."

"There never were," he said. "You still looking for Heathcliff?"

"No. I'm looking for you."

He bent to kiss her once more.

"You guys need to get a room," Garth said, walking to the computer panel. "No one wants to see that beast naked."

"I do," Maggie said, eyes glued to Thad's face.

"I don't have time for this," Garth said.

"I won't be gone long," Thad said, leading Maggie out the garage door.

"Then you're not doing it right," Garth called after them.

Maggie grinned.

They reached the top of the knoll above the creek. The long grass below bent to a gentle breeze. Maggie's legs stopped moving. Her heart contracted.

She couldn't do this.

"I've got you," Thad said, but she'd donned her turtle shell and she wanted to crawl inside.

"I'm going to do everything in my power to keep you safe from here on out, if you'll let me," he said.

"I-I-I'm such a c-c-coward," she said, her voice strained. "I-I-I c-c-can't." She turned to walk away, but she'd turned into his chest. A warm, comfortable chest where she buried her face, inhaling sand and stone particles and fabric detergent and a scent that was all Thad.

She turned toward the creek and drew a deep breath. "My mother always said, 'we must raise girls to be brave, not perfect.' I know I'm not perfect, and right now I don't feel very brave."

"You're not a coward. You have every right to be afraid of what happened to you there, but as long as I'm with you, no one's ever going to hurt you again." Standing behind her, he wrapped his arms around her. "I'll hold you until you feel safe again, and you will feel safe again. I'm the coward. If I hadn't been afraid, you might not have…"

She whipped around and put a finger to his lips. "Not your fault." On tiptoes, she raised to kiss him once more. "Let's get this over with."

They did a sort of gallop down the steep hill, past the oat grass and around a knoll to the bench where once he'd made her forget everything but the way he felt. She shot a glance to the tall grass where his sister had interrupted them, and then she turned toward the path beside the creek that disappeared under the canopy of trees to join the bike trail.

Maggie wrapped her arms around herself to ward off the chill.

"You don't have to do this today," Thad said.

She shook her head. "No, I do have to." The group sessions had taught her one thing. In order to take away the power of those memories that haunted her, she had to face them down. She'd taken baby steps—walking out of the house alone, walking the block alone in Foxfield. This was her final demon, but she was freaking out.

She faced Thad once more. "When you made love to me here, when we almost..." she glanced at the spot in the grass once more. "Were you thinking of Ginny?"

He rubbed a thumb across her jaw. "Truth?"

She nodded.

"There isn't room for anyone else when we're together. You aren't like anyone I've been with before. With that being said, I will admit it brought back memories. Did I think of her? Yes. But later." His gaze moved to Maggie's hair as he smoothed it. "Those memories reminded me how different you are from her, and how much you mean to me." He winced with the words, as if they cost a great deal for him to say.

Maggie took his hand, meeting his gaze. "No more ghosts between us," she whispered.

He nodded, and with a gentle hand to her back, directed her down the dirt path.

Her body shook as if the earth itself was trembling. Heart pounding, arms tightly folded across her chest, she walked into the shade of the trees.

225

A hand on her shoulder…

"Don't touch me!" she shrieked, shrinking away. It wasn't Preston who'd touched her, it was Thad, looking frightened and unsure. She swallowed the fear that coursed through her.

"Maybe you need more time," he said, his voice calm and sure and steady.

No. She was here now. She took another deep breath and held a shaking arm to point out the spot. "He was waiting for me. There." Maggie squeezed her eyes shut, saw the hate in Preston's eyes. Felt his cold, hard lips, and she spat again in remembrance. Without conscious thought, she did the same thing she'd done that day and ran through the trees to the bike path on the other side. In the sunlight, she raised her face to the sky to soak in the warmth.

"I won't let him hurt me anymore," she said half to herself. She looked back, still not sure Preston wouldn't follow, and saw Thad, maintaining a measured distance and watching her like she might self-combust.

Mr. Do-Gooder. Trying his level best to do the right thing, and doing it all wrong. She turned her back on him and wrapped her arms around herself once more. She bowed her head, fighting the tears, the terror.

Two strong hands rested on her arms, his strong body nestled against her back. Thad. Maybe he wasn't doing it all wrong after all. She turned to face him, and held him as tightly as she could, drawing on his quiet strength. His arms wound around her and he rested his chin on the top of her head.

"You're okay, Maggie," he whispered to her.

She nodded, at the same time wiping tears against his shirt, which muffled her voice. "I don't want to be alone tonight."

"Stay with me. I've got you, Maggie. I won't let you go."

No, Thad was doing exactly the right thing.

Chapter 31

Maggie woke up alone in a familiar bed. Thad's. She took a moment to stretch, smiling. He'd been patient and gentle and understanding until she'd finally relaxed in the strength of his body.

She leaned on her elbows. Where was he? "Thad?" The motion dislodged a note on his pillow. Maggie picked it up and read it.

Didn't want to disturb you, you were sleeping so peacefully. Had to go to work. Call me when you get up. Love you, Thad.

She touched the words, her heart swelling. "I love you, too," she whispered.

After a quick trip to the bathroom, she returned to the bedroom to retrieve her phone from the nightstand and glanced out the window.

Woods. She was alone.

Panic welled in her chest.

Silverware clanked in the kitchen. Water ran in what she presumed was the kitchen sink.

She *wasn't* alone.

Maybe Thad hadn't left yet. A quick glance at the phone told her it was after nine. It couldn't be him in the kitchen.

She was *not* leaving this bedroom.

Hands shaking, she pressed her back to the wall and dialed Thad's number, praying she'd hear his phone ring in the next room.

It didn't.

"Hey beautiful," he said when he answered.

"There's someone here," she whispered into the phone.

"Oh, honey. I'm sorry. I didn't mean to frighten you. It's my mom. I didn't want to leave you alone and I asked her to stop over, but I didn't think of it until after I'd left. It's okay. I promise."

His mother? Maggie cracked open the bedroom door and peeked out. Seated at Thad's kitchen table was a woman with shoulder-length black hair, highlighted with fine strands of silver. Maggie closed the door as quietly as she could and drew a deep breath. She glanced at the shirt she was wearing—one of Thad's—and searched the floor for her panties. "She's going to know I spent the night."

"You did say you were okay with going public, didn't you?" he asked, a teasing note to his voice.

"But she's your mother," she said as she yanked those panties on.

"And I'm a grown-ass man. Pretty sure she's going to be more excited you're there than judgmental, if that's what you're worried about."

This was not how she had hoped to meet Mrs. Benson.

"Are you awake, dear?" Mrs. Benson asked quietly. "I heard the toilet flush. Thad said I should let you know you're not alone."

Maggie closed her eyes. "What am I supposed to do?" she whispered to Thad.

"Go say hi," he said. "She's dying to meet you."

Maggie disconnected the call, took a moment to compose herself.

Clothes. She should put on clothes.

"Maggie?" Mrs. Benson said again, closer to the door.

She was a mother, and if she was anything like Maggie's mother, she was going to open the door to check on Maggie. That's what mothers did. Might as well get this over with.

Maggie opened the door. "G-g-good morning," she said. Damn her stutter.

Mrs. Benson gave her a quick assessment and smiled. "I'm Claudia Benson. Thad's mother. I'm happy to finally meet you." She drew Maggie into a hug.

Not what Maggie expected.

"Can I make you a cup of tea?" she asked. "Sandra sent me with a box of blueberry. She says it's your favorite. I've heard so much about you, so when Thad asked me to stop over, I jumped at the chance. I hope you don't mind."

Not trusting her ability to speak, Maggie nodded. While Mrs. Benson put a mug of water into the microwave, Maggie checked the t-shirt again, clearly several sizes too big and hanging to her knees.

"You'll have to forgive me," Mrs. Benson said. "What with running a family business, I've kept my family closer than most, and I tend to be clingy with my children sometimes, to their detriment I'm afraid."

The microwave dinged and Mrs. Benson extracted the mug, adding a tea bag and setting it on the table. "Can I make you breakfast?" she asked.

The whole scene felt surreal. "Not quite yet," Maggie managed, easing into a chair.

Mrs. Benson took a sip from her coffee mug and studied Maggie's face, increasing Maggie's discomfort.

"You're such a lovely woman," she said. "I hope you don't mind me being a meddling mother, but it's obvious how much Thad cares for you."

Maggie bit back the nervous giggle that threatened to erupt. She took a sip of her tea. "I care for him a great deal, too."

Mrs. Benson relaxed and smiled. "I'm so glad. All his life he's heard people saying awful things, like he has a face only a mother could love. I'm afraid he took those comments to heart. He might not ever make a living in Hollywood, but he's a good man."

"Yes, he is," Maggie said. Torie had commented on Thad's looks, too. Was that why he'd closed himself off all these years? Why he was a confirmed bachelor? Because he didn't think he was attractive? "He has uncommon looks. Striking. Does he take after your husband?"

Mrs. Benson's eyes welled with tears. The chance Mrs. Benson was also pregnant was slim. What had she said to upset the woman?

"Yes, they all favor my husband, with the lighter hair and the light brown eyes, but they each look like themselves. Brian probably takes after me the most." Mrs. Benson hastily wiped at her eyes.

"Thad's never shared much of his private life with me," his mother said. "That man owns my heart, you know. Mothers and sons, they say. Oh, I love all my boys, but Thad has always been so quiet. I guess I've always worried a little more about him. When he asked me to stop over this morning, I couldn't pass up the opportunity to get to know you. I can't tell you how happy I am he's found someone he can open up to."

She could say that while Maggie stood before her, barely dressed and wearing Thad's clothes.

Maggie's mother would have made her opinions about spending the night in a man's bed known, despite Maggie being a 'grown-ass' woman.

"I haven't let you say a word," Mrs. Benson said, straightening. She wrapped her hands around her coffee once more. "Tell me about your family. Your job. Something to shut me up and help me learn more about you."

"I was born in Indiana," Maggie said, suddenly thinking of Steve Martin in *The Jerk*. She chuckled and continued. "My parents are still there. I have two sisters. One lives in Foxfield and the other in California." She took a sip of her tea, inhaled the aroma. "And I stutter." Something she'd lived with all her life, along with the judgment. She'd learned long ago to disregard those people who judged her by her speech, so why had she mentioned it?

"The girls," Mrs. Benson speared Maggie with a glance, "that would be Sandra and Amy, tell me they hardly notice it."

And yet they'd mentioned it.

"I'd also heard you had an unfortunate incident recently," Mrs. Benson went on. "My son is a force to be reckoned with, you know. He can protect you from people who mean you harm."

"Is he bullet proof?" Maggie asked flippantly. She sighed. That was uncalled for. "I'm sorry. I'm used to taking care of myself. I know how strong and intimidating Thad can be, but at the end of the day, if someone is intent on harm, they'll find a way." Her own words sunk in.

They'd talked about this subject in her therapy group. She'd obviously been listening. Maggie carried pepper spray in her purse now, and in her hand when she was alone. She'd taken the self-defense classes years ago which had proved invaluable when she'd been confronted by Preston. She couldn't avoid someone who meant her harm, but she could put up a good fight until help came along, and she could be aware of where she was and take the proper precautions so that trouble wouldn't find her.

"Have you had breakfast?" Maggie asked.

"Yes, I ate at home this morning. Can I make you something? Eggs? Pancakes?"

"I was thinking we could walk over to the café and grab something there," Maggie said. "If you'd like to join me." She glanced at her clothes once more. "After I get dressed."

Mrs. Benson's eyes filled once more. "That would be lovely."

Maggie drained her mug. "Thank you for the tea. That was very thoughtful. I'll have to thank Sandra, too." She rose from her chair, and when Mrs. Benson also rose, Maggie reached over and hugged her. "This isn't the way I'd hoped to meet you, but I am glad you're here."

Chapter 32

T had set down his tools to retrieve his buzzing phone, a group text from Sandra.

Maggie's at the café with Mama Benson.

Group text? Thad checked the other recipients—Amy and Garth. Amy was already headed for the door when he reached the showroom.

"And where do you think you're going?" he asked her.

"We can close the shop for half an hour," she said.

"And if she doesn't want a crowd of people around her?"

Amy stopped, set her hands on her hips and stared him down. "You're going, aren't you?"

"Yeah, but I have a reason to be there."

"As do we all, big brother. You're not the only one who loves her."

Thad blinked, and Amy laughed. "Ever heard the phrase actions speak louder than words? Your actions are screaming."

"Still not going to talk about this with my little sister," he said.

"Really? I thought we'd gotten past that."

He cracked a smile. "Some things aren't meant to be shared."

"I'll give you that one." She held the door open for him, flipped the sign around to the clock that said "back soon" and followed him out, locking it behind them.

Together they walked to the café.

Maggie hadn't sounded pleased when he'd told her his mother was there, but he wasn't sorry he'd sent his mother over. After the way Maggie had reacted on the footpath to the creek yesterday, he wasn't taking chances on her having an anxiety attack from being left alone, and with all the new business Benson Monuments was getting, he couldn't afford to miss a day. Not right now.

Garth was already there when they arrived, leaning against the counter flirting with his wife. Amy went to join them, but Thad headed for the booth where Maggie sat with his mother.

"So glad you could take a break," his mother said. "I hope you can convince this lovely woman to stay."

Was she going to leave? An earthquake shook his heart. "Everything okay?" he asked.

"You might have given me a little warning," Maggie said between bites of omelet.

"We've had a lovely time getting to know each other," his mother said.

Maggie reached across the table for his mother's hand, smiled as she squeezed it, and took another bite of her breakfast. That was a good sign, right?

"I was worried you might be uncomfortable when you woke up alone," he said.

"Which you know I was, based on my phone call to you." Maggie took a drink of her orange juice, watching him with something close to amusement in her eyes.

Still a good sign, right?

He turned to his mother. "Is she leaving?" he asked.

His mother faced Maggie. "Are you, dear?"

Maggie didn't reply. She glanced between the two of them as if she wasn't sure how to respond.

"I'll get myself another cup of coffee," his mother said and excused herself to join the rest of the family at the counter.

Thad slid into the seat beside Maggie. "You okay?"

She nodded. "Seems as if group therapy helps, after all. Not perfect, but I feel like I had a breakthrough this morning."

"And my mother?"

"She's a lovely woman."

"But?" he invited.

"My mother wouldn't have been so gracious if she'd gone to my house to babysit my lover." She lowered her voice to the tone that lit him up inside. "Does she do that often?"

"Oh, Maggie," Mrs. Benson called from the counter. "I already told you, he's never shared his private life with me before."

"Would you be more comfortable stepping outside?" Thad asked Maggie.

"Like in the alley?" she asked, brows up.

Trick question. He studied her a moment, trying to decide what the right answer was, and then pressed forward. "No. I think everyone knows we're an item by now which, by the way, makes me look that much better for having won you over. I thought you might prefer a little privacy."

She shrugged. "I think that went out the window when your mother found me wearing your t-shirt this morning."

Was she mad? "I'm sorry."

"The note," she said. "Did you mean it?"

Thad concentrated, trying to remember what he'd written. "Which part?"

"The last part."

His name? And then he laughed at being so dim-witted. "Yeah, I meant it." And there was that stab in his chest again. Had he screwed things up by telling her?

She stared at him, an expectant look in her eyes. Thad sat back, watching her. She didn't want him to say it out loud, in front of everybody, did she? Her brows went up, a clear indication that was exactly what she wanted.

"Here?" he said quietly.

She scowled before she pushed her eggs around her plate.

"You're not a troglodyte, for the record," Maggie said, loud enough for Amy to hear. "I happen to find your face fascinating."

Her words washed over him like a warm summer shower. "I love you, Maggie." He leaned toward her, took her chin in his hand and kissed her.

"I love you, too," she said quietly.

"Stay with me? Marry me?"

Behind him, he heard a thud, followed by Garth saying, "ouch."

"That's romantic," Sandra said.

"Please say yes," Amy said.

Maggie grinned. "You don't mind that I'm a stutterer?"

"Will you listen to that nonsense," his mother said.

"I did give you the chance for privacy," Thad said, still waiting.

Maggie wrapped a hand around his head and pulled his lips to hers. "Marry me back," she said, with barely a breath between them.

"It's a deal." He kissed her, long and slow and deep.

Amy was sobbing again. His mother was murmuring comforting words. When Thad turned to look at them, Garth and Sandra were mooning over each other like newlyweds.

"Don't you have work to do, slacker?" Thad said to Garth.

"As much as you do," Garth replied. "Sometimes there are more important things. About time you figured that out."

"Yeah," Thad said, probably looking just as moony at Maggie. "You might be right."

Dear Reader:

Thanks so much for reading this book. If you enjoyed the story, I hope you will encourage others by "liking" my books on Goodreads.com and everywhere the option is offered, and by posting an honest review to the site where you bought this book and/or at other book blogs/reading sites so you can help other readers decide whether it's worth their time. Authors like and need to get feedback to make each new book as good as it can be.

—Karla Brandenburg

Karla Brandenburg